FILES OF THE

HEART

FILES OF THE
HEART

(a novel)

Iwu Jeff

WORDS
RHYMES &
RHYTHM

Printed and Published in Nigeria by:
Words Rhymes & Rhythm Limited
Suite C309, Global Plaza Plot 366, Obafemi
Awolowo Way, Jabi District, Abuja, Nigeria.
08169027757, 08060109295
www.wrr.ng

DEDICATION

To the members of my world;
For a oneness so strong
And a difference so great
For a path opened
And a bond bottled in sweetness
On my heart's pages will
Your names be engraved with gold
For a lasting memory
Knotted in purity

If I can stop one heart from breaking
I shall not live in vain;
If I can ease one life the aching,
Or cool one pain,
Or help one fainting robin
Unto his nest again,
I shall not live in vain.

– EMILY DICKSON

'Women empowered'
Is millions helped
In the home
At work
Equity should be
The game
This must be
The maxim
In Africa,
Everywhere.
'Power to the Women'

– AKACHI ADIMORA-EZEIGBO

Cold light of the day

CHAPTER ONE

Her eyes became round; restlessly pawing the air with fascination. She fidgeted and her eyes moistened, but the tears were hidden in her heart. She was frantic and couldn't look at the audience. She became red; her eyes blinking on and off. Her fists were clenched and her eyes, fixed at the ceilings. With each blink of her eyes, it seemed like the world hardened against her. Tied were her hands and her tongue too. One would say she had been counting the ceilings. True, she counted and counted again- the ceiling lines, with her focused eyes and churning stomach. A feeling of excitement blended with fear stood growing inside her, from her belly to her gullet.

She became still- very still! Standing on shivering legs, her mind lingered on those things - the things he had told the audience about her. Was it not a thing of joy? Was it not expected to rhapsodize her? Within her was a runnel of peace flowing surreptitiously in felicity. Her mouth was heavy; as heavy as a pile of rock. Too heavy to spill words; too heavy to break the calabash for the world to see. It was just too heavy! It had been planned. Yes, it had. Had she not known? Was her mind unconnected to this planning?

She just needed not to say, 'no'. Even if she did, would it be taken for an answer?

The fear of what tomorrow could bring made the tortoise to take its shell along to wherever it went: an adage she recalled, prevalent among her people. What was she to fear anyway? The sweet or bitter experiences of life? To her, it had been a muddle of both, growing from innocence to this present state- living objectively and trapped by life. She was just beginning to understand what it meant for life to be *unsugared*. But she must pretend. That was the general rule. No one must know that a running stomach troubled the king.

She stood glowing in agitated happiness; beaming with bright-red lips that exposed whites that gleamed.

***

It was a Sunday afternoon. The sky was bright and sunnily dressed in crystal apparel. It had that appearance which put smiles on the faces of the city's busy inhabitants. Not that moody look that often resulted into frequent downpours that drenched the city; beating it black and blue and leaving it afterward to the overwhelming power of murky waters that formed stagnant ponds and oozes. Just last week it had rained five days nonstop. The city of Eyimba was painted red in the solemnization of the holy matrimony- Obinna Udoka and his bride Nwakego Amadi. 'Just wedded', tagged the silvery decorated Honda CRV jeep which conveyed the couple from the church to the reception hall. The hall was alive; buzzing with different kinds of music. The most popular one was *Flavour's Ada Ada*.

Applauses erupted, filling the hall with sounds of approval. Such applause as never heard before; it came from the guests. Could it possibly be sounds of disapproval? No. The smiles on their faces could never betray their thoughts. All the guests rolled in the aisles of laughter. A jocular but sensitive question had been asked by the master of ceremony and the groom's response had been jocund. Such question made the guests amazed and amused. The groom had responded from his heart- he had poured out his piled up emotions. What was there for him to hide? Nothing. Was it not said that a truthful person must not be killed? They must be spared to live for the truth lives till ages.

Obinna stood boldly. His muscular body that accommodated his broad chest and shoulders was the focus of the audience. He was tall. He stood *gidigba* like an *iroko* tree. His fair skin shone brightly in the hall. Had the lights ceased, his skin could have illuminated any darkness there.

Obinna had said it all. And that was it. Now were they all ears to hear her response?

The young woman stood motionless; joggling and staring at the guests with much agitation. She was enthused, a myriad of thoughts flowed in and out of her. Positive thoughts as she had never imagined.

She was perplexed. She just found it hard to fathom the rationale for his unprecedented action. She had seen so much dexterity in what her brother- Obinna had just told the guests at the wedding reception. Obinna has done it again; she muttered.

With a grin, she strained to speak. Her voice was unsteady. Her feet were shivering before the guests. 'I'm Chinwe- his sister. He has said it all. In my whole life the one I would like to thank most is my brother . . .'

She was interrupted by a wide applause that rumbled side by side like thunder. In that happy occasion, tears rolled down her powdered face like an oil drip.

Chinwe walked down to the floor ponderously. She thought of why her brother had kept an ace up his sleeve in remembrance of their childhood experience.

So he had everything written and stored as files in his heart? This is a record of life- a record of events which would forever be engraved in my heart with gold. What more could one be asking for but for a beloved like you- Obinna? What? Chinwe thought endlessly. The words of his speech kept on reverberating in her mind. The old story he told was like a recorder played back to her. Bodily, she was present but absent minded.

My sister...my sister...yes, Chinwe -my sister! When we were in primary school, our school was in a village very far from home. Every day, my sister Chinwe, and I would walk to school and back home. One day, I lost the other pair of my brown sandal; my sister gave me her own sandal to wear. She trekked the long school distance barefooted. It was indeed a dense sunny day. Getting home, her legs were swollen because of the long distance she trekked. She couldn't wear shoes for two days . . . I made a pledge on that day that as long as I live, I would love and take care of Chinwe, my sister. I would always be good to her.

That was what Obinna told the guests.

Did she not also fight for him that day? Chinwe did. She fought for her brother; that kind of fight which kids often get involved in on their way from school. She was so protective of her brother. That was many years ago. Long, long ago. She had not been cut off from him to dwell in blurred memories.

A bigger boy had stopped them on a bushy path that led to the village stream. The boy's name was Okenwa. School children called him *Iburibu*. That was because he was fat and too big to be in the same class with the little children of Obinna's age. He was a threat to the children. He would involve the small boys in an argument which often heated and led to fights. Iburibu would often beat the children in class and would also wait for them on bushy paths to begin his troubles with them.

Chinwe and Obinna plodded the narrow path as they were returning from school. The path was overgrown and winding. Tall trees stood left and right like giant soldiers arranged for war, with bushy grasses making powerful canopies that prevented the sun from shooting its hot rays. They couldn't see far ahead neither could they see far behind. They heard coughs ahead of them. 'Yes! Now we can continue what we started, *gbo*. I have you here now, all to myself! *Akwa gi-* you, no one can save you. Not even your sister,' Iburibu said jumping down from a thin branch of an *Udara* tree. His Igbo dialect was strong and deep. One could tell from his voice that he had not been exposed to civilization. He was a stark villager. Raw. Though he was in school, he was still unrefined. He had that malicious voice that threatened smaller children. It made the children believe they could never stand him in a brawl. This made him a village champion. *'Taa! Taa!* Today is your day! I will teach you to respect your senior,' he moved towards Obinna, 'I'll teach you what the *arushis-* deities, do with the sacrifice of chickens.'

Obinna ran. He hid behind Chinwe. 'Sister, he wants to beat me!' Obinna screamed. 'Who's he?' asked Chinwe.

'He's the big boy that always beats us in class!'

'Gini - what did you do to him?'

'Onweghi- I did nothing to him. He's the boy I told you about. He likes beating us, just for no course.'

Chinwe stood looking at Iburibu. She could be threatened by his size. She looked at him from head to toe. His body weight alone could weigh her down. It was enough to make her groan like one pressed with force to pass away hard faeces. Now other children were passing by. They all stood to watch the drama with fear for Chinwe and her brother. But Chinwe gained confidence. She ignored his size. 'What did he do to you?' she asked Iburibu.

'I must beat him. And if you don't release him to me, I'll beat you too,' Iburibu boosted.

Chinwe guessed Iburibu's intention. 'Come then and touch him if you have no fear in you- *bia!*' she drew a border line on the ground using her leg. 'If you know you sucked your mother's breast cross this line. Come now!' she sneered.

Iburibu was bold and arrogant. He stepped into the border and faced Chinwe. 'So, you're really here for trouble,' Chinwe faced him eye to eye. The number of children there had increased. Iburibu tightened his fists about to hit it hard on Chinwe. He missed his target. She was so smart that she discovered right away. 'Is that how it is?' Chinwe retorted. 'I'll teach you a lesson, *taa!*' She released a slap and it landed, sounding like gun shot on Iburibu's right cheek. One could see the stars jumping up and down in his eyes. He lost his balance. Chinwe was fast. Before he could retaliate, he was sized up by Chinwe. She pushed him down and he fell to the ground like a leaf.

Chinwe was on her knees as she pulled him on her shoulders and flung him on the ground repeatedly... Now, Obinna ran to aid his sister. They both fed his mouth with sand. Filled and filled to the brim. That was the yardstick for determining a winner when kids fought. She had won the fight. A girl won!

Iburibu lay on the ground wriggling in a ferocious tantrum. He was so weak now and ashamed of himself. The children rejoiced and laughed; falling from left to right like tree branches dancing to the tunes of the storm. Iburibu had always been the village champion. He was defeated and shamed by Chinwe- that little girl whom he could ordinarily threaten with his body. An ordinary girl, he thought. Were it to be a male- a fellow male like me, it could have been a different thing. Never! Not me, Okenwa- the Iburibu that is feared by everyone in this village. He remembered the words his father always said- *never underestimate the power of a woman*. This is true, Iburibu concluded with shame knowing the humiliation and affront that awaited him from friends.

Chinwe was hailed and raised shoulder high by the children. It was always fun when in such rare cases a female defeated a male in a battle. Such a male would get a title, *Onye ome ngwu*- a weakling. And, the female? She would gain the status of *onye ike*– the strong one.

Obinna turned to Iburibu, '*Nmee! Ntoo!* Come and beat me!' he charged. The children sang- *Chinwe onye mmri! Chinwe onye mmri!* From that day, Iburibu stopped bullying other children at school. The class rooms now dwelt in serenity devoid of Iburibu's troubles.

Chinwe smiled after remembering that event. It was an event that asserted in her a sense of authority- the authority of a female over a male folk. So a female folk could defeat a male in a brawl? This erased from her mind the belief that women must remain with arms folded to become objects subject to torture and psychological disposition. Robots! Controlled with a remote! To her, women were the people objectifying their fellow women. She swelled in pride.

That was the same day she trekked on bare feet. As Chinwe pondered on those words her brother had said, she became more languid. Her mind wondered touring into the stoic conditions Obinna had been passing through in order to see her head raised above the waters.

But why did the master of ceremony ask that question? Why? Is this kind of question asked in a wedding reception? So, it was planned – Obinna had it worked out. These things went on in her mind blithely.

She sat with her husband Frank; a man of thirty five who appeared to be in his teen. His slim body made him appeared younger than his age likewise his bright face which was neither folded with wrinkles nor coloured by pimples' dark spots. His chin had no beards. Each smile he released had innocence coated in it. Chinwe and Frank appeared gleeful in their sparkly ornamented lace apparel of white and purple. They were filled with life. They were on a gleaming high table sternly decorated and reserved for the guests known *as 'very important people* (VIP)'. But Chinwe was so heavy like a trip of sand. Her mind was suddenly recuperated later. It was a joyful event. Joy made an abode in her heart at the mid of events.

As she sat twisting her body and legs on the floor to the rhythm of the music played, her mien automatically changed. She was so rhapsodized. The expression on her face changed. Music had been a healing to her soul. With a large grin, she rose up from the seat and drew Frank by his hands, *'Nkem, nkwa,'* she called and headed straight to the nuptial dance floor where the bride and groom where staged for dances. They jived widely to the sound of music played.

The dance floor was at the stage. The couple danced with ease in gyration as the large guests watched. Suddenly, it became a relish in overkill as members of the high tables and other floor members stepped into the dancing scene. They danced in exoneration with the wedded couple.

As the music became magnified, the hall and the people in it were made sprightful. They flung crisp Naira notes at the couple. Chinwe couldn't think about the happenings again. She danced with frank and would later face Obinna and Nwekego.

The reception ended with jollity. The guests all celebrated and wished the couple a happy home in their union. They all returned to their tents with their minds bubbling with joy.

Chinwe still had her mind ruminating on the event- her brother's love was never to be compared to any. Frank watched her. She was moody. Was it not an ordinary wedding reception? Was it not a thing of joy? Why would her mind be set still on the issue? These and other thoughts competed for Frank's attention. He knew something was wrong with her. And what that could be was totally erased from his mind.

CHAPTER TWO

The night was engulfed by quietude. Though she slept on the bed in her husband's arm, she considered herself solitary in the room. She rolled from one side of the bed to another keeping awake but oblivious of her surroundings. Inside her was a growing turbulent of thoughts. She arose and hissed. Her hissing was deep and loud. It sounded like the hissing of a snake. Frank was deeply asleep. He neither turned nor woke to the hissing sound she made.

She sat by the edge of the bed and watched intensively like a spy, the velocity of frank's snoring. She muted a thought in her mind with her eyes fixed on him:

He is here like the log
He sleeps like a goat
He snores in his sleep
The sound of his snore
Like the tidal wave;
He's gone deep to the world
Sent he by nature.
Wide open are my eyes
With my heart filled to the brim with
thoughts.
Take he no cognizance of
My vigil? On his lips
Are written this love for me.
In my troubled state

Does he find rest
Yet he claims he loves me,
Can he ever love me more
Than my brother?
At my brother's love will
My heart be at rest.

The room was dark but the reflection of the lights through the window brightened it a little. Lights penetrated through the white transparent curtains. The quietude of the night was broken by the cry of the night birds. The dogs outside barked so fiercely. Their awful and repeated barking made her tremble. Even the evil spirits would be trembled by that. She could also hear the wall clock tick- tacking in its regular night duty.

Chinwe stood up, walked round the room, and pressed a button on her mobile phone which displayed the time boldly across the screen.

'It's a new day, 12:00am now? How long can the night be? An impish night awake, vied in duties with the night watch like a dog...' she muttered.

She stood by the window, opened the curtain, and gazed at the sombre night which was brightened by the lights outside. Their flat was upstairs so she was able to clearly see the Ariaria road that was silent like *ikpa*. Colorful lights shined from the buildings and they made everything before her seem like a beautiful landscape. A painter might be tempted to make a canvas painting of Faulks road at night.

She stood for minutes with her tongue and mind tied tightly. Could she have said a word when the walls have ears but cannot speak?

She turned back, watched frank on the bed and with a tiptoe she trudged out of the room. She gradually jammed the door behind her. Through the passage she headed to the sitting room; walking on the tiles which were as white as the pulp of a washed cassava. Her footsteps neither slapped the floor nor made a *tam-tam* sound.

She sat on the sofa. Her legs were stretched beside her. Her right hand was placed on her curved jaw. She had her mind crowded with a countless number of thoughts as those words she said at the reception reverberated against her ear drums. Her lips shook and grasped as she spoke to herself: 'In my whole life, the one I would like to thank most is my brother . . .'

Chinwe took a deep breath and slowly stood up. She slightly stopped. She moved on again and stopped. She took few quick steps towards the light switch. She put on the light. With her finger still on the switch, she looked at the big wall clock which had a wooden frame and a silvery jingling bell.

'Hmmm! God!' she released a sigh with a deep breath. She switched off the light and wobbled back to sit on the sofa. It was twenty minutes past twelve.

As she sat there, she saw her brother's image present in her mind. She saw him in his ideal muscular nature. She looked straight into his eyes: 'I love you brother. In my whole life the one I would like to thank most is you, my brother . . .' she said.

***

The night suddenly became cold. Torrential drops of water fell from the sky. The light's reflection went off immediately power was cut by the electric power authorities. Gloomy was the sky and the darkness of the mortal abode was like a black charcoal. That darkness was thick and tangible with no trace of glimmering light. The sky released its drizzle which made choruses on the roofs of mortal buildings. That was just the beginning of the mid night cold.

Albeit the night was cold, it was as if a heap of heated coal was burning inside of Chinwe with hotness. Her mind travelled to all directions of the earth.

Her life had been as she expected, courtesy of her brother who had sacrificed a lot for her. But she was unfulfilled yet.

Had Obinna the power to make me a fulfilled woman, he would. Why is my own life different? I wish...I just wish this cup will come over me! She murmured. What then is the joy in marriage when there is not even a single fruit to show for it?

Chinwe hardly thought about her marital problem. But that night she thought about it. Was it not said that thought leads to thoughts? Frank had been helpful. He had told her never to be grieved by their marital challenge. Had he not also told her that options existed as solution to this? She had been mute.

Nne- Frank's mother was not helping matters at all. Had Nne not developed a sudden hatred towards her- Chinwe? Her constant visits and presence were now turning the house into a house of brawls- the gathering of cat and rat. Chinwe was just beginning to understand why most of her friends in the university prayed to get married to men whose mothers were dead. These friends of hers had rejected many suitors just because their mothers were alive. To them, mother-in-laws were nothing less than witches. They would bite a rod to make a home inhabitable for their daughter-in-laws. To this new generation of women, mother-in-laws were tagged to be; *high blood pressure*! *Stinging Scorpions*! *Serpents*! Cynthia, her best friend had joined this league of ladies who prayed and wished the death of their prospective mother-in- laws-before their arrival into the family home. To Chinwe, that was evil. But, she was beginning to see a ray of light in those prayers and wishes. Why?

Had Nne not visited a month ago with her trouble? She had arrived that evening and Chinwe had felt like the ground should open to swallow her up. There had been a knock on the door. Chinwe had hurried to open the door and it was none other than Nne, her mother-in-law. She was a small woman. She didn't look so old but almost all her hairs had turned grey and her breasts sagged limply.

Chinwe embraced Nne, giving her the normal brief side hug. She smelt strongly of *azu ndu*- ice fish. That was what she traded on in the village. All her clothes now clung strictly to this smell of fish even though she had been away from it, preparing for this malicious visit. Not even the strongest *Hausa* perfume could emit this odour.

"Nne, welcome ma,' Chinwe greeted. She added, 'how was your trip?'

Nne didn't reply. And this time Chinwe could smell trouble all too much. 'Nne, you didn't even tell us you were coming. You should have called us so we can prepare well for your visit.'

'*Oyanu!* That is it! I knew it! I said it! So, I can no longer come to my son's house except I write an application letter?' Nne screeched.

'No! *Mbanu*! It's not what I mean *Nnem*! It's not like that,' Chinwe replied.

'It's not like that,' Nne mimicked. 'How then is it? School woman! I said how then is it? I told my son about you school people. But he wouldn't listen. May *amadioha* the gods of thunder rumble on you! In fact, the thunder that will fire you is still preparing...it is pressing up and down, waiting to shatter your head to pieces!'

Frank heard the quarrels and came out. '*Nnem*, welcome. How was your journey?' Nne didn't give a reply. '*Nnem*, you've really changed. *Legodu!*' Frank smiled broadly. He continued, 'You didn't even tell us you were coming...'

'I said it! I said it! May *amadioha*...may *ani...*' she paused and continued. '*Legodu*, see what this school woman has turned my son into. *Chim*, see! My enemies have really succeeded by giving me a witch for a daughter-in-law. They have also turned my son into a *she-man*! My son can no longer stand again as the man he is. Now, my enemies want to send me out of my son's house,' Nne surly cried. She walked and sat on the sofa with her hands placed on her head.

'*Nnem*, what is the meaning of this?' asked Frank in a shrill voice.

'Meaning of what? The meaning is that my enemies will never succeed in making you childless. I'll dig deep to the root of this. I must send this witch out of your house and bring to nut all her charms and concoctions against you. Didn't I tell you never to marry a school woman? These school girls are witches who in their schools hunted for men and slept about, involving themselves in all manner of abortions. Some of them even remove their wombs in the process,' Nne cried out more loudly.

'Stop it! Stop it! Nne, is it not God who is the giver of children? Does He not give at his appropriate time? If He doesn't give us then we seek for an option. We adopt!' Frank said.

'Abomination! *Aru!* It will never happen in my life,' Nne jumped up and moved to face Chinwe. Chinwe was as calm as a lamb. 'My son will never adopt for you! Not in this life. Not when I'm alive. He will never pick any child from the gutter. He will never pick any child given birth to in a baby factory by prostitutes like you.'

Chinwe burst into tears without a word leaving her mouth.

Nne continued, 'my son will never pick up such children. Not when his manhood is still alive and strong like a rod. No one ever adopted in our family. I told you my son. But, you wouldn't listen to my voice. These school girls, do we not know them? All they do in school is to hunt for men at night- witches! They sleep around sucking all men. They involve in all manner of abortion. Some of them even remove their wombs. When they go for their *corper service* that is when they become worst. My son, no man who wants a family would marry a school girl who has even gone for *corper service.* I told you! Now, tell me young woman, how many abortions did you commit before trapping my son in your web?'

'Nne, it's alright. Please stop,' Frank pleaded.

'Stop what? Stop *gini*?' Nne questioned. 'It's never alright. This school girl must go. This witch must leave. I'll do all within my power to send her out. My *chi* will never make me childless. I must dig deep to the root of this. My enemies will never succeed. I will get rid of her charms and concoction. Let me ask you, hope she hasn't sucked you dry yet? Hope you can still perform? I pray she hasn't made your rod weak. That's what these witches and goal diggers do!'

Frank and Chinwe couldn't release any word; they stood still watching Nne who burst into a song: '*onye biara abia ga alala, onye biara abia ga alala!*'

Tears gathered in their eyes, but they didn't let them fall. They were stored in the mind instead.

Chinwe had all these revoked in her mind. She often champed the events of the past like a goat with four stomach compartments whenever she was alone, and at each time it made her cold. She had always been obsessed about issues revolving around her. Now she became totally lost. Lost. Lost in her turbulence, the thought evoked in her a casual curiosity.

Suddenly, there was a flash of light in the sitting room. She sat still on the sofa with her hands triangularly placed on her jaw. She was engrossed in her deep thoughts. She couldn't hear the sound of walking feet or perceive the presence of a being. She was far away. She was touched by a being; mortal or immortal? Scared! The feeling made her cold. It covered her with goose pimples. Her head began to swell to an unimaginable size with her heart jumping out from her mouth. He tapped her. She was dismayed. His hand was as cold as water in a clay pot. She returned from her journey, shivered and turned to discover it was just a tap on her back. The dogs barked again and again, they must be barking at the passing of some cacodemons whose duties were to torment and inflict pains on innocent mortals and to cause them nightmares.

'*Nkem,* what are you doing here?' Frank asked in a low voice.

Speechless, she stayed for some minutes and brightened her face slightly with a grin.

'Searching the flies of my heart,' she replied.

'What could that mean?' he questioned.

She turned to him. 'Where the heart is driven away the body stands still . . .'

Frank moved to her direction, he sat with her on the sofa and patted her back. 'Speak to me, I know you are with a laden heart, I can see the lacuna inside of you. Is it all about the incident at the wedding? What more could it be?'

She readjusted her sitting position and coughed out loudly.

'My heart has searched out the tales of old hidden in me that my mouth is too heavy to tell,' she answered.

'Tell me this story dear, my ears itch to hear,' Frank coughed out. 'I know he loves you, right from the first day I saw him; I saw the existence of true love. I discovered the bond between a brother and a sister. It's extraordinary, I see.'

Suddenly, an owl hooted with a frightening loudness right at the top of their roof. The crickets' heartfelt songs became louder, but this was usual. The owl hooted and hooted again. The hooting of the owl was terrifying, it sounded like a ravenous bird of prey, ready to devour. This owl must be evil, Chinwe thought. For some days now, it has been hooting constantly at the roof of this house. Was it not said that an owl only hoots repeatedly on the roof of the house to which evil must befall?

Scared! Chinwe clung to Frank. He held her in his arms but in her was a roaring echoes of fear clothed in gloom. Her mind was in shackles. Yes, shackles- evil was knocking at the door. Her shackled mind once again grew with wrestling thoughts and fear which clobbered intensively.

'I'm terrified,' she said.

'Such is it when one is enslaved in the cells of sleeplessness at night, the sounds of the night creatures make you feel the presence of a monster,' Frank replied.

'Yes, it may be. But I feel happiness in this terrific sleepless night, within me is the flies of old stories. My heart is too heavy for my mouth to tell parts of the story; can I ever forget the trails of my brothers scratch of love? Does a thought not lead to thoughts?' Chinwe said looking deeply at Frank.

As she became absorbed in her outpour of feelings, drops of calmness like drizzles began to soothe her agitated mind. At this time, a melodious sound came from the big wooden wall clock and was preceded by a *'Gbam! Gbam! Gbam!'* sound. The clanging clock alarm broke the silence in the dark room.

'It's 3:00am,' Frank said.

Chinwe was hushed. Frank quickly stood up and drew her up immediately. 'You need to sleep now. In fact, you must sleep now! You can't continue staying here thinking all night about your brother's scratch of love.' Frank said as he led her up from the sofa. She smiled and followed him. As she stood up, the room was instantly bathed in light. Power was just restored by the electric power authority. That had been the habit- on and off; playing with power. Just two days ago, a four-storey building had been set ablaze as a result of this inconsistency of power. It came on and off.

Frank held her firmly in his bosom as they walked back into the room. Her mind bubbled in happiness; she burst out into a heavy laughter as Frank touched her.

When they entered their bedroom, frank headed to switch off the air conditioner. The night on its own was extremely cool; mortals could be frozen to ice by it. She lay on the bed and rested her head on his chest like a baby. Afterwards, they wrapped themselves with a heavy blanket and minutes later, they succumbed to nature's plea for sleep. They slept like logs, completely oblivious of their surroundings.

CHAPTER THREE

The morning cold tied hands and feet indoors with its freezing breeze. It made the sandy mortals unaware of the crack of a new dawn, but at the watch of the weather no one would sow or reap.

Outside, the city bustled with lots of activities though not in its usual time. It grew with humming sounds of vehicles by motorists, horns of motorcyclists, noises of conductors seeking for passengers, sounds of traders and hawkers heading for the search of daily bread at the famous Ariaria market which had gained international recognition in the Eyimba city.

Chinwe and frank just woke only to discover the fast hands of the clock in a competitive race. The sleep at the early hours had changed her therapeutically, giving her a grinning countenance. But those enigmatic thoughts of the night were yet to be erased from her mind.

Could she be untied to lay bare these files of her heart? Which was she to talk about? Her brother's love story? Her five years marriage which was almost crumbling? But she had found so much attachment to Obi. So much that couldn't be untied from her. Obi. Obi meant so much to her that she wouldn't make play of him.

She stood up, watched the time, 'It's 9:00am,' she noted inwardly. Her mind travelled the regions of the earth: East, West, North, and South. The events of her fresh age flashed across mind and she ruminated on them.

She went to Frank and peered intensively into his eyes. Her eye lashes stood, fluttering in a manner that couldn't be interpreted. She became unconscious as her mind took her to Umuozo, her provenance. She sat down with frank by her side.

***

It had all started at a very tender age in the village, Umuozo, a beautiful but small and isolated village attached to the Eyimba city. The village presented its inhabitants with a breath of pure fresh air. It dwelt more in serenity at the rainy seasons. The fields of the village were often filled with smiling crops and flowers, with trees weaving to the breeze. Small birds filled the ambience with their chirpings. Though attached to the city of the Eyimba, the village had no presence of city life in it; life there was a tranquil place with little or no sounds of scooters, motor-rickshaw, and motor-horns. Nature made its beautiful abode in Umuozo – a rural verdant life reflecting nature's beauty.

Chinwe was three years older than her brother, Obinna. She was the first child of Maazi Udoka. Maazi Udoka loved his wife, Mma Nwanyi, whose parents named *Mma Nwanyi* (a woman's beauty) as a result of her irresistible beauty. She was terribly beautiful. She was the most beautiful in the village during her days. She never passed by without getting the attention of all; men and women. With her beauty, she gained a new name during her youthful days; *Olu gbajee*- breaker of necks. People of the village were astounded at how she shunned her numerous suitors, clinging to Mazzi Udoka; a poor village farmer and hunter. He fondly called her Mma (beauty) as an expression of his love for her. He had always protected her from falling prey to men and strangers in Umuozo.

Their marriage yielded two fruits – chinwe and Obinna after seven years of childlessness. Maazi Udoka and Mma had visited several *dibias* to find solution to their childlessness but all to no avail. At the sixth year he had urged his wife to trust in *Chukwu*- the supreme God, who is the giver of children and at the seventh year she conceived to give birth to chinwe. They called her Chinwenwa - God owns and gives children. This was to prove to the world that God the creator is the owner and giver of children.

After three years, Mma gave birth to a male child which was celebrated by the family and was called Obinna by the father. Obinna – the father's heart as called by the father meant to prove that it was God's desire to give a son to the family again after three years of chinwe's birth. The children grew up to love themselves.

***

A trend had just risen among damsels; the growing girls of Chinwe's age- that awkward age when their bodies seemed to be sugared for sweetness. That was the age in which young girls were said to have their bodies doing them *Pauli-Pauli*. This trend had come from the main city and was like a harmattan wind blown into the village. All the girls at her age seemed to have it. Chinwe admired and would like to have it. She often stood at a vantage to have a cursory look at the girls with this. It was called the 'vandan' by the youngsters.

The *vandan;* a red squared handkerchief dotted with white flowers, it became a requisite for knowing the growing damsels in that awkward age. Chinwe couldn't wait to have it.

That day, she had just stolen fifty naira from her father's drawer. With the money burning a hole in her pocket, she headed straight to purchase the *vandan* in order to join the train of girls in the village. This however put her nose out of joint as her father discovered the stolen money right away.

Chinwe and Obinna were made to kneel against the wall. Maazi Udoka held a bamboo stick in his hand. The sight of the stick boggled them; they were not unaware of the crime that had been committed. Is a guilty conscience not said to fear no accusation?

Obinna knew what had happened to the money. Chinwe had a bogey of guilt burning like a conflagration inside of her.

'A man who walks alone carries a load of palm-fronds,' the children often said to each other, especially when one desired to be protected by another. Chinwe and Obinna did all things together; good and bad.

'Who stole the money? *Onye?*' Maazi Udoka vociferated.

Chinwe's eyes turned red. Her face became like the roadside faeces stoned with a catapult. She didn't call tears to gather in her eyes. They came uninvited by the bearer. The situation of event had invited the tears, willy-nilly. Stunned and too afraid to speak, Chinwe's lips shook jerkily as a stream of tears flowed down her cheeks from her red eye balls. The tears descended to wet the earth. She prevaricated as she watched Obinna intently. Neither of them admitted to the crime.

'*Mba*- no! 'It's not me!' Chinwe cried.

'I'm not the one!' Obinna said.

'This is inglorious!' Maazi Udoka screamed. He added; 'Fine, since none of you wants to admit to it, you both must be beaten up. You are learning bad manners every day. But you must know that anyone who urinates in a stream should be warned because any of their relatives may drink from the water. Our examples are like seeds on a windy day, they spread far and wide.'

After addressing them in taciturnity, Maazi Udoka lifted up his hand tactically. With the bamboo stick in hand, he grabbed Chinwe with his left hand. As he was about to hit her hard, Obinna vociferously cried out aloud; 'Papa, I did it, I stole the money! *Ommu! Me!*'

'*Gini?* You? Bad child!' Maazi Udoka said.

Maazi Udoka at this point stood still with his hand raised up. Chinwe shivered in apprehension. Maazi Udoka booed and walked around, left and right. His teeth were set on edge. His hackles were raised to the highest. He sprightly smacked Obinna's back repeatedly. He lashed him until he lost his breath.

At the end of the whipping business, he sat down on a stone and had him scolded. 'You ought to be beaten to death. A dried fish can't be bent. If I don't bend you now, you will remain unbent forever. If you learn stealing from your own home, what other embarrassing thing will you not do in the future?' he said.

Maazi Udoka narrated the story of a boy to his children:

'That was how Innocent, the son of Mbonu started stealing right from his father's home. He started with the stealing of meat from his mother's pot of soup. His mother and father neglected him. *He is only a child; he would change,* so his parents said. He moved into another level- stealing his father's money from drawers and yet he was neglected. The boy saw stealing as a normal way of life and as such went out with the habit into a small scale stealing enterprises. When he graduated from that, he became a professional armed robber. He later combined robbery with kidnapping for ransom and that was the last straw that broke the camel's back. He was paraded alongside with his five accomplices. They were said to have abducted a popular man in Ohaozara and later killed him at Nguzu Edda forest. It was reported that they also engaged in drug peddling, taking cocaine from Brazil to some other countries in West

Africa. When they were arrested, the law caught up with them and they were brought to book.'

He hissed. He added another louder but slow hiss which this time sounded like a deflated tyre before continuing his sermon. 'Did you not also hear the story of the boy-Chika who became a thief? When he was about to be killed, he requested to see his mother. His mother was brought to him and he asked her to come closer. When she came closer, he chopped off her right ear with his teeth. He confessed that at his tender age when he started stealing, his mother never corrected or scolded him. He that has ears let him hear now – the world wouldn't say I did not speak! I've spoken. I'm speaking. I'll keep speaking. Let the world hear me now!'

After the narration, Maazi Udoka talked nineteen to the dozen for the whole day.

The day ended and the evening came. Mma, the children's mother came back from the *Afor* market and the events of the day were narrated to her. Her hair didn't stand on end. She added fuel to the children's burning fire. She severely harangued them for their act. She afterward drew the children to herself, hugged them, and wiped away their tears. She touched Obinna whose body was now stippled with wounds. Obinna never shed a single tear. Mma's act was however in accordance to the saying: 'Beat a child with the left hand and bring him back with the right hand.'

Mma never vaunted any of her children, especially when they did something bad. She had always encouraged them to be veracious at all times. She instilled discipline into them.

At midnight, Chinwe couldn't sleep. She voiced out her piled up emotions; crying. Obinna didn't let their parents hear her crying. That could be worst for her.

'Sister, cry no more, whatever that happened has happened.' he said.

'I couldn't admit what I did...I hate myself for my act of wickedness. You received a punishment I was supposed to receive,' Chinwe replied.

Just as a scar can never be healed, years went by but the incident grew fresher in their minds. It was as if it happened yesterday. Chinwe did not forget her brother's act of protection. She kept it to heart. That year, she was eleven years old while Obinna was eight years old.

CHAPTER FOUR

Years went by. *After a coon's age, the sleeping dogs had been left to lie.*

Chinwe and Obinna were now through with their secondary school education at the community central school. In fact, Obinna had been very fast, he had finished at exactly one year after his sister.

An idle hand is the devil's workshop. Chinwe knew very well that she would be made slack by idleness if she did not engage in any fruitful thing. For her, staying at home doing nothing was not an ideal thing. At the drop of a hat, she had collected a meagre amount of money from her mother. She was able to start up a fruit-selling mini shop at their veranda. She would go to Umuozo fruit market to buy fruits and would return to sell them.

With the profits she made, she was able to fend for herself and some of the family's needs. Her mother had taught her that a woman needs to be hard working in order to meet up with family challenges. She had been told by her mother that a lazy woman only sits to eat from the husband's treasury and afterwards makes her husband bankrupt. Chinwe made herself venerable through hard work and diligence. She would like to experience self-empowerment. She had heard so much about it. Mma was already rearing her for this. She wouldn't like to be that over dependent house wife-*obiageli aku*. No man marries a liability as a wife again; Chinwe thought. To her, liability wives are those who contribute nothing. No economic or intellectual contribution. They just stay at home to gratify their men's erotic desires. Do they not end up becoming reproductive machines; dropping fruits annually? These kinds of women grow older than their ages. They are consumers. Parasitic wives! This really has to end; Mma often said. Women must contribute actively in family and social development. They must free themselves from every shackle that limits them- they must never be objects for erotic gratification. Never! They must make themselves intellectuals too. Who said they can't be?

Chinwe had saved some money with which she registered for the Jamb university matriculation examination. She made the examination and was ushered admission to study her desired course in the university. She slimed herself to bone in order to raise her head above the waters with no fiasco. That was her mother's belief. Her principle. Success only comes to the prepared hands.

Obinna made nine passes at the West Africa school certificate examination. With hope, the family had planned it that he would sit for the Jamb examination in the following year after Chinwe.

Now that the two birds were striving to move to the higher level of their education, the economic situation of the family had sternly became ferocious. What could the parent's do, having two of their children heading to higher institutions?

***

That night, the cold grew feral. The silence of the night made it possible for the hearing of approaching footsteps of any creature. One could hear the creeping of the insects. The moon stood, shining brightly with millions of stars dotting the sombre sky above in the cold night.

Maazi Udoka squatted in the yard smoking packets of cigarette. He had just returned from the evening hunting exercise with his friends. They had caught nothing; the animals were indoors giving warmth to themselves, clinging to one another as cover. So, they did not come out and mortals had caught nothing.

There in the yard, his wife, Mma, sat very close to him watching. He stood up and moved closer to a bamboo slat in front of the yard. He stood motionlessly and absent-mindedly with his cigarette in his hand. He paid total attention to the sounds of the night's silence.

He looked up at the sky in its gloom and saw millions of lights in their pulsating blinks. He couldn't unravel the night's mystery. The moon itself stood in the sky spreading itself like a mat in its squeezed elaborate beam of light. The moon was seen as a piece of yam in the sky. It scaled steeply in the roofs of the village buildings ostentatiously making lengthened shadows of nearby trees and standing humans. It also served as light to the path of bare footed night passers-by who treaded the silent route to the farms and streams in the summer. This nature's creature enticed the soul of everyone with the striking sublime of serenity in nature's aestheticism.

The children were always excited to have the moon. This piece of yam in the sky was made specifically for them by *Chukwu*-the creator. The full moon at night gave the children a reminiscent of the twilights. They usually felt a special stimulation which jerked them out of maudlin stupefaction. It often gathered them to the village square where an elderly person would come out to tell them the tales by moon light. They were told tales of old which exposed them to their past, tales of adventures, tales of animals as well as didactic tales that developed high moral standard required of an African in them. They also learned virtues and skills needed as nuggets for life. Riddles and jokes were not excluded from the moon lights' activities.

As Maazi Udoka stared deeply at the lights, his mind was casted to the events he participated in during his childhood days. Those events were activities of the moonlight.

'It's black when unused, red when using it and grey when used, what is it? The charcoal,' He remembered this riddle as well as the story of the tortoise which was famous during his time as a child.

The tortoise was considered wise by mortals- most cunning of all the animals. It was a period when fruits were yet to ripe on trees - the tortoise was seen climbing a tree with many unripe fruits. As the other animals saw him, they hysterically laughed at him, 'you foolish Tortoise, why are you climbing a tree with unripe fruits? Don't you know it's not the season for ripening of fruits?'

As they laughed and mocked him, the Tortoise replied, 'Don't worry, by the time I get there, the fruits would be ripened.' While the other animals continued to pillory the Tortoise, he undauntedly continued climbing the tree. Moons pass after moons, Tortoise finally got to the top of the tree. Everything in life has its time and season. Lo, it was the ripening season and the whole fruits were fully ripened. Tortoise didn't look at the other animals, he started eating and enjoying all the fruits alone on the tree. The other animals were perplexed, they bellowed as they waited in vain for the fruits to fall to the ground. *Success indeed comes to the prepared hands!*

As Maazi Udoka remembered this story, he smiled. He interpreted it in his mind. You might be climbing the tree of your destiny right now in life and people around you may neglect you. They may be laughing at you but don't worry because at the appropriate time, you will finally get to the top your tree. Those who pilloried you will be ashamed of themselves- Maazi Udoka thought as he continued in his deep thought of the night. *Success only comes to the prepared hands!*

The night also served as a sweet moment for lovers. The men often hid themselves at the tree trunk. They stayed there to sing and play serenade for their intended spouses during courtship.

❈❈❈

Muffled with silence, Maazi Udoka had millions of ideas running through his mind as thoughts. With his cigarette, he rummaged on the thoughts. He had just returned to his conscious state.

He was puzzled. He wondered what could be done now that the children were at the tip to climbing the next ladder in their educational pursuit.

Chinwe was inside the room. Her ears were sternly connected like a satellite to the arena where her parents were staged for the night. She eavesdropped at her parents' conversation. She could hear her father ask her mother, '*Nkem*, our children have good results, what can we do?'

Mma couldn't utter a word. She gave an unconscious sigh that echoed in the cold night and sounded like the buzzing of bees. She was deeply saddened by the statement. She had often considered the economic situation of the family and each time she conceived and nurtured this within her she felt sudden cold mixed with perplexity. This cold often raised the pores of her skin, making her hairs to stand erected like the hackles of an angry dog. As she pondered over the situation of things, a pool of salty waters flowed with currents out of her eyes down to her cheeks desultorily. Her mouth grew heavy and tamed. Finally, words let go off her, dropping like an ice from the sky. She said, 'What is the use of their good results? How can we possibly finance both of them?'

Tranquility reigned at the compound for a couple of minutes; neither husband nor wife could break the silence. Of a sudden, Obinna zoomed in glaring at his father audaciously. With him the long lasting silence was broken. In his tenacious self-decision he stood like a lion in front of his parents. '*Nnam,* I don't want to continue my study anymore. Papa, I have read enough books, my sister can continue, she's a girl,' he said. He added, 'girls should be allowed to go to school at this time. I'm a man. I can succeed even without education. Have we not seen many men who are successful without much education? *Adannem*, can acquire much education and be the light in the family and in the husband's home too.'

Maazi Udoka stood up. He watched Obinna with his eyes burning furiously in anger. That was an aggravating and grilling statement. He imagined, what could give Obinna such impetus to make such an impious statement? The boy is beginning to grow tail. This tail of yours must be cut- yes. It must be cut so that it doesn't grow into something else; that which could look like a snake. An animal is better tamed at its young age. I must cut it. I must do my duty as the man of the house. I must man my home well before another does. I can do this by cutting and cutting these children's tails- what else have I got besides them? I must.

Cut the tail. Cut it now! Cut. Cut. Cut. He dwelled in deep thoughts. He swung his hand and slapped Obinna's face.

'Why do you have a spirit so damn weak? Why do you always do things that are a bit close to the bone? The spider that knows what it will gain sits waiting patiently in its web. The praying mantis is never tired waiting all day. Even if it means I would have to beg for money on the streets or knock at the doors of my adversaries, I would send you and your sister to school until you have both finished your studies. Your sister has gained admission; she would go first before you. All you need to do is to wait for her till next year *inugo?*' Maazi Udoka said.

Chinwe watched her brother and out of solidarity she piteously walked to him. She struck out her hand as gently as she could to his swollen face. In low pitch, she bellowed as she spoke to him. 'Sorry, papa is right. A boy has to continue his study if not he wouldn't be able to overcome the poverty we're facing today. Education is the weapon which emancipates the poor from the shackles of poverty. As the man of the house, you must go to school. I'm a girl, I can get married, be in a man's house and all he needs to do is to take over all my responsibilities. I can sacrifice for you. Take the exam; let me continue waiting till I find a man. I have decided not to continue my study at the university again,' she said soberly.

'*Mba!* You must continue. You have to go for your desired course. You have to be empowered for the task ahead of you. I see you going places...when someone like you is empowered it is millions helped,' Obinna replied.

Chinwe and Obinna stayed all through the night being saddened by their rock-like inflexibility. But Obinna's mind was already made up and he couldn't count the cost of his intended action. He stayed awake in daze thinking about Chinwe's education. What was he to do about it? Something had to be done quickly.

CHAPTER FIVE

The sun rays peeped through the windows into the room where Chinwe lay on the bed, revealing the crack of dawn. Though had she slept late, she had a fairly good night rest.

She woke up to discover that the day would be over taken by the scorching sun in place of the incessant rain. Her mind grew spirited and frenetic. This was because a sunny day would give her patronage in her fruit selling business.

She rose from her bed, plodded round her room, headed to the curtain, and opened the window to ascertain the time of the morning. She smiled elaborately and thought of planning for the day's activities. The twinge of the night and its features had surreptitiously vamoosed from her mind.

Today would be fruitful, she thought hopefully. Since she left the secondary school, she had learned to use her mini business as a cushion to the financial situation she found herself in. She didn't make play of her business at all. She grappled it without complaints. She would do all the necessary chores at home after which she would purchase fruits from the far market. She would amble from the market with a laden bag of fruits which she often tied in enormous bundles and placed on her sinking head.

Chinwe smiled again. Sunny days made her euphoric unlike rainy days that shatter her schedules and leave her with no profit but loss and waste.

In her stream of consciousness, she wobbled to search for Obinna. Now, the thought of the night's winged words flashed into her mind.

She called with a voluble babel, 'Obinna! *Obim*! Where are you? *Bia biko* – come please.' Her Igbo language sounded deep. She often spoke with that deep accent whenever she had a gossip to tell.

She left the room and meandered around the compound. She couldn't find him. Where could he be? It's too early for him to go out, where has he gone to? She cogitated. She went back into the room quivering.

Obinna had left the house before dawn without anybody's knowledge. He had thought that his stay at home would make him run around like a headless chicken. He wouldn't like to toe the line of his father. He had left to grant his sister the opportunity to continue her education. He believed so much on this *empowerment* thing. *When a girl child is empowered, millions of people would be helped-* that was his belief. He had heard that over and over from his school teacher while in the high school. He wanted all concentration to be on Chinwe during the course of her study. He wouldn't want his sister to be in that group of women tagged *liability* wives. So, he must leave.

He left with few pieces of worn out clothes. He had clumsily sneaked to chinwe's side of the bed and slipped a note beneath her pillow.

He wrote on the note: '*Sister, getting into the university is not easy, I will go and get a job, and I will send money to you. Go there to be empowered!*'

Chinwe read the note in a wink of an eye. With her eyes fixed on the paper, a body of water formed like a rivulet there. She let the waters down to her cheeks and they broke off into tributaries. She forlornly cried until she lost her voice.

***

Obinna's departure made news. It spread like harmattan fire round the village of Umuozo and its neighboring hamlets. Maazi Udoka sent three young men who were members of their clan, to engage in a rescue mission, to search for him.

Mma must not know about this. She mustn't detect that her son was missing.

This issue was hidden like a skeleton in a cardboard from her for three days.

The news would make her hairs to stand on end. She was hypertensive and her condition had often worsened at points when ill issues about her family flittered into her ears. Everyone in the family avoided to lay bare to her Obinna's departure.

She had fainted and was hospitalized at the village health centre one time where she was bedded for three days. She had been placed on sedative drugs by the doctor. This was at the time when Obinna fell from the top of a mango tree and sustained broken arms. The knowledge of this had bedeviled her. It had placed her under a critical condition for days.

'They've killed my son! My enemies are at work. *Chim,* don't make them succeed. My only son. *Otu anyam-* my only eye. My pride- my enemies: *ndierom!*' she had wailed then.

No one would accept to be causation of her hypertension. No one. Not with this very news of Obinna.

She often asked after her son but all she got were prevaricated responses. Flimsy excuses were given to her in order to calm her down with silent hope that Obinna would be seen after the long search.

After three days Obinna was still nowhere to be found. They had even gone to

Osisioma and its environs. Finally on the fourth day of their search, Obinna was seen at Uratta junction leading to Ariaria market, at the Eyimba city. He had joined a group of hustlers at a construction site where he was actively engaged in labour, mixing cements and carrying blocks. His father joined the three men to plead with him to return home. He was told that his long stay would compromise his mother's health.

Obinna's love for his mother made him return but on a condition that he would continue working at the construction site on a daily basis.

Mma was not told all these. Missing Obinna for three days had been an illness to her but on seeing him, she felt recuperated. The family's bogy was finally allayed. 'May my *chi* never allow my enemies succeed in any of their plans. I'll never become a laughing *stock* for my enemies. Empty-handed they came, empty-handed they'll go. *Ndierom gbara aka laa,'* Mma prayed and the family echoed, '*Iseh!'*

Light in the tunnel

CHAPTER SIX

However long the moon disappears, it must shine again someday.

Chinwe had nothing else to think, dream and fanaticize about except the day she would go into the university to start her course. The thought of other things had served as a pale junk to her.

She had suddenly become capricious and apathetic towards her business. She would often sit at her veranda to day dream and create mental pictures of university life. She thought about the friends she would make, the trendy life of campus damsels and the general gusto attached to campus fun.

She had visited the university a week ago and fed her eyes with the most attractive areas of the university. She just couldn't wait to explore those beautiful areas.

She glared at the humdrum village. 'What am I still doing in this village? When will I finally leave this local place to enjoy the campus life?' she often asked herself.

***

Chinwe finally left for the university she was admitted into to study business administration. The university and its environs filled her with gaiety. She had saved some money with which she paid her steeply fees which included registration, tuition, and accommodation fees.

Every member of her family had contributed charitably to see that she left the home to begin her studies. Her mother Mma had given her widow's mite.

Just two months ago, a woman had met Mma, asking her why she would allow her only daughter to be a school girl. The woman's name was Nwachi. She was known all over the village for her garrulity. It was said that her husband had left her for another woman due to her lack of tongue control. People often brought bad reports about her to her husband. With her tongue, she had divided and destroyed many homes. She would creep into the homes of young couples to set the husband against the wife, and wife against husband. It had become a saying that anyone who paves way for Nwachi into their home paves way for division and unbridled hatred. Nwachi was considered to be *onye ashiri*- a gossiper.

'Why? Why do you want your girl to join those groups of prostitutes all in the name of school?' Nwachi asked. 'You left your son whom will inherit your family and you decided to raise another man's wife...'

'No! *Mba dada*! Everyone needs to be trained. Tell me *dada*, have we not always complained of not having a say in the issues of our land? Have we not been subjected to the floor by our society- the men? How can we be free from these if our daughters continue to remain in this dark tunnel, unexposed? Unenlightened? Not empowered? Are they not the leaders of the future? Our future. Your future...' Mma explained.

Nwachi cut in. 'Do they not go there to become irresponsible? *Ndi akwana-* prostitutes! They become disrespectful to all-elders and husbands. They move about testing their strengths on the phallus of all men. They know every strong and weak rod possessed by different men. Tell me, how can such women settle in men's houses? Do they not allow their door holes to be free for all keys? That is all they learn in those schools. The worst happens when they go for this their so called *corper service*. Mma, if I were you I will not allow my daughter into this,'

'Don't say that. We can't be the same. A bad tree is known by its fruit. When we help them, we help ourselves, we help millions,' Mma replied.

'But that's the truth- yes, the bitter truth. It is in those schools they learn to be disobedient to their parents. They choose any kind of men for marriage instead of the men often chosen by the parents. Tell me, during our time was it done that way? They learn their strong-headedness from the white men,'

Mma laughed out loud. She was bent by her laughter. 'But that was then! Things change day-by-day. A woman should be allowed to select her own man. My father knew this and as such, I was permitted to select my man amidst many suitors. I wished I had the opportunity to go to school too,'

'School? Thank your stars you never did. I'm sure you could have been worse than these school girls you always support.'

Evil woman, Nma thought as she smiled. She roams about like a lion seeking for homes to devour. She is set to steal, kill, and destroy homes. Your venomous fruits of hatred, I shall never eat from.

She smiled again with her thoughts unpainted on her bright countenance which revealed beautiful dimples on each side.

'Didn't you hear about, Nneoma the wife of Ukah, she was beaten black and blue by her educated daughter-in-law? What then is the fruit?' Nwachi asked.

'Nneoma's case is different. I'm not in support of the young girl's attitude in anyway. But Nneoma has been so cruel and wicked to that young woman ever since her arrival into her son's house. Are things done that way? No! Was it not also reported that sometimes she beats or slaps the daughter-in-law. Nneoma is known for troubles, everyone knows this,'

'Was that enough to justify the girl's action?'

Mma dimpled a grin, not of glee but of anxiety. This anxiety was coated like a sepulcher by her words and hidden expression- indifference. '*Dada*, you won't get this answer from me. Tell me, how would you feel if your own daughter is treated just the same way Nneoma treats her sons' wives? If such is done to her daughters, how would she also feel? A balloon explodes when too much air pressure has been blown into it. Mothers must treat their daughters-in-law well for peace to reign. No woman is born into a man's house. Everyone inherits from another. Today it is me in the family house; tomorrow it would be my daughter-in-law. Let's keep training our daughters,'

'*Nno nu*. May your efforts be fruitful. To me, no son of mine dare brings in a school woman into my home. School girls are terrible. They're disrespectful. They're wild and rude. They argue a lot. Before you say a word, they've said fifty words. They bark too. No daughter of mine goes there to join them,' Nwachi concluded.

'Can you hear yourself, *dada*? Aren't we the cause of our problems? We often blame men, claiming they're the engineers of our family and social crisis. I've observed that as women we need to work on ourselves.' Mma said, shaking her head from left to right.

✻✻✻

Obinna had also given Chinwe some amount he raised from his hard labour for her university education. Their father couldn't save enough money so he had to borrow from his three friends whom he promised to pay back within two months.

Mazi Udoka was addled as to how to raise money for Chinwe's departure but in adagio the thought of meeting his three friends whom he had helped at one time or the other cascaded his mind. He called them to his home one evening; an evening when the golden sun receded to kiss and welcome the full moon into the night duty.

Seats were brought out that evening in the arid compound. Mma had prepared a sumptuous meal which she served her husband's friends with fresh palm wine. Maazi Udoka chatted with them during the dinner after which he started his plea for aid.

'My dear friends, our people said that a good friend is better than a bad brother. When an only kola nut is presented with love, it carries with it more value that might otherwise be associated with a whole pod of several kola nuts. I'm at the tight corner of life. May I not be drenched by the murky waters that fall from the wicked clouds. Just as a single man does not build a house, one finger can't remove lice from the head...' He explained the condition he found himself in. And his friends; Maazi Udenba, Maazi Okafor and Maazi Okoro had unanimously agreed to requite him of his good deeds.

'It's a man that scratches the back of another man; to the tree does a goat run to have its back scratched, but a man runs to his fellow man. Our dear friend here has been very nice and keen to us. We can't leave him now to sink in the river of adversity. Chinwe his daughter is also our daughter. A child belongs to all and not to the parents alone. *Ears must we all be to him now!* We have all heard his pleas; we all must put our hands together to raise this child. Remember that we would also join the parents to enjoy her price when her market comes. We will all enjoy the dowry together with the parents,' Maazi Okafor said to the other friends.

'*Eziokwu*- true, she's our daughter. She must be prepared to stand firm in order to fit into the current society. We all must never follow the old ways. A new order has been made for us and our children- male or female must not be denied this,' Maazi Udenba said.

'Yes! That's true!' Maazi Okoro concurred.

'Who knows the man that would come for her tomorrow?' Maazi Okafor said.

'Yes! *Ndi obodo oyibo!* People from abroad!' shouted Maazi Udenba. This shook Maazi Udoka. It nauseated him and he jumped to his feet, '*Tufiakwa!* Not my daughter! No child of mine will go to a white man's land with a man I don't know!' His friends were all surprised to hear these words spilling out of his wide mouth.

'Why?' Maazi Udenba interrogated.

'Aren't they the genesis of our problem? What is so special about them that our people swarm there like flies drawn by *nsi*- faeces? Did we not learn that most of our young men are there suffering?' Maazi Udoka replied wistfully with a sigh and scratched his chin.

'My father told me what those men in pig's skin did to them. How they turned them into slaves. How they even respected ordinary *nkita*-dog, more than them-humans. How they humiliated and ridiculed them, bounding them in shackles like criminals, making them trek under the scorching sun- dried and squeezed, and discolourated, passing through a land they know as *land of no return*, into the great ocean. They made them suffer to death working on plantations; empty. Tell me, a man who has no respect for your father, grandfather, your ancestors, what does he have to offer you?' Maazi Okoro sharply asked.

'*Oooh!* Our young men can succeed with or without them. Do not some of them slave for them in their land? They become mere cleaners, gardeners, cooks and they even wash the white man's undies...' Maazi Udoka said but was sharply interrupted by Maazi Udenba.

'May my *chi* forbid! No son of mine would go there just to be a washer man for the *Oyibo*. None would wash their undies. Who knows how their undies look like? Do their undies have that brown part that always appears in our own undies? I mean that part which appears dirtier than other parts,'

The men burst into laughter. The laughter floated above their heads.

'Why not? Aren't they mortals? I'm sure they do. Can you ever search the anus of any human – white, black, red, brown, all colours, without finding a fragment of *nsi*-faeces? No!' Maazi Okafor asserted.

Maazi Udoka continued, 'We face difficulties today simply because our people have been so dependent on them. Isn't it better for our boys to be here hunting, farming, or even taping palm wine, than going there to suffer? Instead, they go to become slaves- washers of undies,'

'We're to train our children to learn their ways. To fight against them with their books and pens, yes. We must equip them- male and female. When we do this, we help ourselves.' Maazi Udenba finally agreed.

Without hesitation, Maazi Udenba, Maazi Okafor and Maazi Okoro agreed to contribute a reasonable amount of money. They had considered how good Maazi Udoka had always been to them. They had responded to his clarion call, thus, one good turn deserves another. With the money contributed by his friends, Maazi udoka was able to settle Chinwe to have her legs fixed into the university.

***

Chinwe's legs were fully felt in the university. She out grew the stage where she stood with one leg. With her two legs, she now stood like a fowl which has been used to a place. The thought of her career made her gaily at all times. She had also become acquainted with many people but she often took to heart the words of her parents before her departure from home.

She often regurgitated those parental sermons. 'I know the daughter I raised and she knows her family. I know the seed I planted and the fruit in it. Remember the daughter of whom you are. Represent your family well. A good child is pride to the parents and a bad child is shame to them. Do not allow the negative changes over there to influence you,' her mother had sermonized.

Her father had gone very close to her and humorously drew her by the right ear. 'If one imitates the upright, one becomes upright. If one imitates the crooked, one becomes crooked,' he said.

Walking into the university, Chinwe had her ears to the ground and even in her selection of friends; she shunned all forms of frivolous fraternity. The words of her parents had always flung into her mind in reiteration, hitting like a strong drum in her mind.

In her first year in the university, she had devoted her time to the study of her roommate, Cynthia, who she was age mates with.

Cynthia was an average-sized, slim and fair skinned girl with long ebony hair. People used to say she was beautiful- her long nose, tiny eyeballs and a face dolled up with dimples, really attracted people to her. Cynthia was a student of journalism. Chinwe had stuck to Cynthia like glue.

Cynthia was her only solace and confidant. They often avidly explored their worlds together. Fun was also a match played together by them. She discovered that Cynthia had a sister who stayed in the Northern part of the country; she was studying in a Federal College of Education. Cynthia and her only sister had lost their parents at a very tender age. Life was a thorn and gloomy abode for Cynthia and her sister. Two of their maternal relatives had volunteered to raise and take care of them. Cynthia's sister stayed in the North with their uncle who lived there. Cynthia had always seen herself as a persona non grata but for Chinwe's friendship, light had resided in her smiles of recent.

CHAPTER SEVEN

The afternoon was filled with frantic activities. The sun was angrily kindled to strike the devastated human heads with its scorching hotness. It had chased mortals out of their bases, emulsifying them into the salty waters like an apoplectic goddess in a race against time.

Chinwe had just returned from her lectures that afternoon. She was so stressed. Nature had given mortals a cold shoulder in that anywhere one perched on became so hot. Even the throats of mortals were dried like pan placed on a cooking fire. She opened the door to her room and fell to the spring bed like one stroke by *Amadioha*- the god of thunder. At a wink, she devoured the half loaf of bread which stood in her room like a sacrifice to a deity.

After few minutes, she picked up her book to study. Lying on her bed, she was engulfed and seized by the overwhelming power of sleep. Just then, Cynthia walked into the room and tapped her. 'There's a guy waiting for you outside; a villager!' she said in a tone of gossip.

Chinwe jumped to her feet lackadaisically, yawned, and dithered round the room. She sighed. 'Why would there be a villager waiting for me? Who's the person male or female?' Chinwe asked.

'A male,' Cynthia replied.

'Where is he? What does this villager want from me?'

'He's outside at the lounge. Go and see him. I don't know what he wants, but you need to see him,' Cynthia responded.

Chinwe walked out sluggishly like a sheep. Who could this person be? She thought. She had never received a visitor since her enrollment into the university. No one would look for her; not even a villager.

Bedazzled, she saw her brother Obinna from afar looking grubby. His whole body was coated with dirt, dust, cement, and sand. His shabby outlook was exacerbated by his sclumsy gait. He also acted like a typical villager who stood on a leg in a place he was unfamiliar with.

Obinna had come to visit Chinwe. From his place of work at the construction site, he had boarded a taxi and alighted at the university gate. He had seen a horrible site on his way coming. That was at Uratta road, before Ariaria Junction.

A mob had ceased a man who seemed to be in his forties. A woman in the bus had raised an alarm. *'Onye oshi! Onye oshi!* Thief! Thief!' She claimed the man had engaged in a pick-pocket; stealing five thousand Naira from her hand bag. How that happened was a mystery to all. It could have been a set-up. How was this to be confirmed? Issues like this happen every now and then with people setting up their foes who finally become victims of circumstance. The man might have even done that to save a life. Perhaps, his son, daughter, wife, or anyone was at the verge of death. He might have done that to feed as things were really hard. The man had no one to speak for him.

He was finally searched and truly found with five thousand Naira. He stood there knowing his fate. He shivered. His mouth was shaking as if an electric current had been placed on it. His face changed. He couldn't run. To where? Beside, before, and behind him were touts. They had embayed him like ships in a bay, with clubs. Abuses had been showered on him as if he had done the worst. He had been beaten black and blue. On the hot tarmac he lay helpless under the drying sun like fish left to dry. That was not enough. His fate? Death. Was he not set ablaze?

They had come like good Samaritans; donating tyres, petrol, and match sticks. No one could speak for him. 'Burn him! Burn him! *Onye oshi! Onye oshi!*' the people shouted. Within a wink, the man screamed watching his body turn into ashes. Within a wink too, the mob scattered like seeds blown away by the wind.

Obinna cried. He didn't let down his tears. He hid them in his mind. What was he to do? That man was a son. A brother. A husband. A father. No one could adjudicate him. His life ended on that road. He might have promised someone of return after waving a good bye. But his life was blown away as ashes, like woods. And the woman? Didn't she walk away as if nothing happened? She did. Obinna thought about this until he alighted at the campus gate and scuttled towards it.

At the gate, there were four security guards and two uniformed police men. They stood at the university's entrance; they watched and searched with a metal dictator those who came into the university. In fact, it had become a norm, metal and bomb dictators had been made available at most institutions of learning in the country. This was to avoid and curtail possible risks of bomb explosions at learning centres. Reports by the national mass media had it that explosions were rocking down some northern institutions of learning weekly by some faceless terrorists who were a threat to the peace of the nation.

Just two weeks ago, it was reported that over two hundred girls were abducted at a school in one of the northern states. Explosions were also recorded to have burnt down churches, mosques, markets, and motor parks, leaving many as massacred victims. It was believed that this terrorism in the country could be politically crafted.

Cynthia's sister had called her sister two days ago to inform her that last week a female suicide bomber had blown herself up with a student in an attempt to blow up the college auditorium which was filled to the brim with countless number of students.

The country as a whole now lay shaky in risen dusts as terrorism and insurgency spread like wild fire, leaving the citizens in the shackles of fear. Here and there were rumours of bombing, gunning, and abduction. Everyone had been at alert as the culprits were known not in their faceless faces. This made it stern for all to pass through the search examination before entering into the university. Everyone jumped through the hoops of this recent development.

※※※

Obinna had passed through the gate after being searched. He had followed others who strode in through the open gate. He had wriggled as he watched the architectural designs and the bold lettering which spelt out the name of the university. He stared with peak admiration.

He wobbled long in his search for the female hostel. After wandering for about thirty minutes, he succeeded in locating Chinwe's hostel by running into her roommate; Cynthia, unknowingly.

Astonished at the sight of him, Chinwe fastened her legs like a sprinter to embrace him. 'Why didn't you tell my roommate that you're my brother?'

He gave a broad smile. 'Look at my appearance, what they would think if they know that I'm your brother? Won't they laugh to make fun of you? I'm just a villager; raw and unrefined,'

Chinwe's heart was pricked. She was quiet for some minutes. She stood still as tears gathered in her eyes like a lake of stagnant waters. She quickly swept away every dirt and dust from his body with her handkerchief.

With a lumpy throat, she looked at him, and into his eyes. She said, 'I don't care what people would say. You are my brother no matter your appearance,'

Obinna gave her a brief side hug, dipped his hand into his pocket, and brought out a beautiful hair clip with butterfly designs. He clipped it to her hair. 'I saw all the girls in town wearing this. So I think you should have one,' he said.

Chinwe couldn't hold back herself any more. His account bashed her piled up emotions. She battled to control herself. She pulled him into her out stretched arms and cried, exuding her joy sonorously. Her emotions made her oblivious of the passersby and the ever busy university environment.

That year, Obinna was twenty years old while Chinwe was twenty three years.

CHAPTER EIGHT

The news about the country's chaotic state had spread like wild fire across the globe. Newspapers, magazines, radio and television stations had hit the stride with their captivating captions and these captions had instigated fear in the lives of the citizens and aliens. Every day was like an escape into life from the prison's vault of insurgents. The integrity of the country had been deeply threatened. It was a common saying that the country's politicians had continued to play politics with insurgency in the country, thus fighting it seemed impossible. The insurgents had grown wings and were now flying with pleasure.

All ears had been opened in strict attention to hear and all eyes had been strictly fixed to the papers, all to get the latest information on the events in the country. Everyone was at alert. The hearts of all were melting like the burning wax in the odious hands of fear.

***

Cynthia had just gone to the vendor to get some newspapers. As a student of journalism, she had made reading newspapers one of her hobbies. Getting there, she scanned through the papers and found some interesting headlines. She picked a paper, sat down and flipped through the pages. Her heart hit hard. It hit and hit with the highest beat like the *ikoro* drum.

She found a report said to be submitted to the United States congress by the secretary of state. The report had alleged massive corruption at all levels of the Nigerian government and the security forces.

It stated that the Nigeria law provides criminal penalties for official corruption but the government had not implemented the law effectively. This was why officials frequently engage in corrupt practices with impunity. It scored the judiciary low. It said that there was a widespread perception that judges were easily bribed and litigants could not rely on the courts to render impartial judgments. Citizens encountered long delays and alleged requests from judicial officials for bribes to expedite cases or obtain favourable rulings.

'What! Wonders will not cease to end! What would they do with all this huge money they are stealing? Here are the masses suffering, can corruption ever be washed away from our soil? Has it not eaten deep into the fabric of our nation? They said; *faith is the believe in the unseen-* I believe; let me just believe it will be well...' Cynthia soliloquized and reflected on her thoughts. 'But when? When will it be well? Will it ever be well? Waiting for wellness would be like the white elephant's project...how long would it take to be well? We shall wait and wait. We're waiting. For what? For when things would go well! May our long wait never be like the wait for *Godot.'*

Her eyes narrowed in incredulity and her mouth went agape the instance her eyes caught a hold of something. She read that the estimated government money lost to endemic corruption and entrenched inefficiency amounted to 1.067 trillion naira. The report included many evidences of fraud among the government. It also cited how some personnel in government had stolen 32.8 billion naira meant for police pension fund. It pointed to how four state governors allegedly misappropriated or stole 58 billion naira, 25 billion naira, 18 billion naira, and 12.8 billion naira respectively. Their trials were said to have begun and would continue till the end of the year.

'What trials would continue till the end of the year? Can we ever hear about the case again? The case would just be covered just like the other cases. We did not start reading issues like this today- this is our country; we know what is going on,' Cynthia mumbled.

She couldn't continue reading the papers. She closed them. Reading those amounts said to be stolen or misappropriated made her blood curdle. She took the papers and headed to the hostel.

At the hostel, she met Chinwe sitting on the bed impetuously. There had been a fight in the room. This had been the usual thing every now and then. Three days ago it was between Josephine, a Calabar girl who had been humorously named, *Zuma Rock* because of her backside which she often fluttered around and a Yoruba girl, Bola, who resided off campus. Bola had come to warn Zuma Rock who was said to be going after her Sugar daddy- Barrister Ken, a member of the state house of assembly.

Just this afternoon, it had been Zuma Rock and a girl in the next room, Timi. Timi was a very skinny girl with a face that featured sunken cheeks and a bony jaw line that was ridged. Her body was so shrunken that her friends often compared her to drying sugarcane. She was Ene by name. Her thin stature earned her the name Timi- a coinage used in addressing very slim, thin, or bony persons.

Timi had hopped into the room where Chinwe and Zuma Rock were chatting with neither a knock nor an excuse. 'Where is that prostitute that thinks she owns all the men simply because of her oversized buttocks?' Timi furiously asked.

'What is it? You can't just barge in here to begin to call names! No!' Chinwe vociferated.

Zuma Rock quickly sprung up from the bed where she sat. 'How dare you? When did you start this? Who're you referring to? We can't have you name names here!'

'It's you! You, boyfriend snatcher! See, I've only come to warn you. Leave Chike alone for me. You know he's my boyfriend; you have numerous men perching around you like butterflies. Leave Chike for me. If I see you around my man again, I will deal with you!'

'See who is speaking! So bones can speak. I will just break you into pieces. I wonder what Chike saw in you that made him come to you in the first place. What do you have to offer? Tell me!' Zuma Rock shrilled.

Timi was irked. 'Look at this bitch! It's you who have something to offer? What do you have except this backside of yours that can be shared with five women?' she belligerently demanded.

'Jealousy! Should I lend you part of it? Listen, Chike is mine. I've gotten him. So, you can get another man. I have what it takes to get any man I want, you jealous girl. I smell envy- jealousy!' Zuma Rock clattered.

'Envy? What should I be envy about?' she guffawed.

'My Zuma Rock! Off course, you're envious of my backside which attracts men to me,' Zuma Rock said, moving dramatically round the room. She wriggled her backside, making it dance to an unheard music played by an unseen player. It made that *tapam-tapam* sound; shaking like hot *akamu*. 'I'm sure you've been dying and praying to have it...' she said.

'I don't blame you. You're nothing but a shameless prostitute!'

'How dare you call me a prostitute? I'll teach you a lesson you will never forget in life. I will break you to pieces today,' Zuma Rock echoed. And in a blink of an eye, a slap landed on Timi's face. The slap made a strong *pam* sound that brought in outsiders from the next room.

'You slapped me?' Timi shrilled.

'Yes, I slapped you and I'll slap you over and over again if you don't take your useless and dirty face out of here,' said Zuma Rock. The room galvanized into violence, heating and boiling, and at the apex other girls at the hostel came in to calm the situation. Chinwe also aided, holding her roommate, Zuma Rock. After this, the girls disappeared leaving Chinwe behind in the room.

Minutes later, Cynthia zoomed into the room with some papers. She looked around the scattered room. 'Babe, what is it? This one that everywhere is like this; was there a fight here?' she asked.

Chinwe smiled. 'Yes, it was Zuma and Timi from Room 5. That girl is full of troubles,'

'Well, I'm sure it's the usual boyfriend or sugar daddy stuff they always talk about. Has she snatched another one? That's their cup of tea,' She laughed and quickly chucked the papers on Chinwe's bed. 'I brought you some papers! Read so that you will not be in the dark of events happening in the country. Read so that you would know the evil being perpetrated by the men in power. Read so that you would be exposed to your ignorance, I want you to be a reader; a reader is said to be a leader,' she said indulgently as she walked to her corner.

An American kidnapped in Nigeria: Total war: read the newspaper headline.

Chinwe was enthused to read. The headline had captivated her. Her reading readiness was stirred like that extrinsic motivation which a child gets when promised of a bicycle after a first position in the school end of the term report. She quickly opened the page and it read:

'An American missionary was kidnapped on Monday from a school in

central Nigeria in an area prone to kidnappings for ransom...'

According to the paper, security officials reported that this particular kidnapping was probably not the work of the country's most threatening terrorist group. The commissioner of police said the abductors had demanded for a huge ransom at barely twenty four hours after the kidnapping. He stated that it was not typical of the insurgent terrorist group. Those insurgents would never demand for ransom.

Chinwe hissed. She covered the page. 'May God deliver our country from evil,' she said.

She quickly flipped through the pages. Dazed, she found another story with the caption: *Sixty died and many wounded in Kano bomb blast.*

Chinwe wept bitterly:
> *Blood sucking demons*
> *Rising dusts in the land*
> *The land lies shaky*
> *With their crafted*
> *Terrorism which now spreads*
> *Like wild fire*
> *Now are we awarded*
> *'League of Nations'*
> *In ruthless massacre*
> *In magnitude of evil*
> *Now is our serenity*
> *Turned to chaos.*

Can we ever see their backs?
She stood up with the papers in her hand and as she made to continue to read it, she heard a commotion outside. Her mind fainted. *Gbim! Gbim! Gbim!* Her heart beat started to pound.

'We no go gree oh!
We no go gree!
Fifty thousand!
We no go gree!'

She listened with rapt attention. she heard the voices of students singing furiously. She peeped through the window and saw them in hundreds, rallying. Cynthia came to join her in the peeping.

Chinwe quickly recalled that plans had been on for a protest by students on the sudden increment of their school fees. The fee had been increased from twenty- five thousand naira to fifty thousand naira by the university management. This had raised conundrum among the students and the university. The Students' Union Government had solicited for the reduction but the university insisted on having their way.

The protest started at exactly 12:00pm that Saturday. A countless number of students barricaded all the strategic areas of the university with abandoned metal drums, tyres, vehicle parts and tree branches. They had chased the university security guards and the armless police men away from their stations.

They matched violently in unison with their song:

> *'We no go gree oh!*
> *We no go gree!*
> *Fifty thousand!*
> *We no go gree!'*

The university officials had heard the protesters and had all hidden in their abode as if they had heard the saying: *'to your tent oh! Israel!'*

The angry students had trapped all vehicles belonging to the university and every other vehicle seen inside the campus. As they moved, they sang angrily round the campus.

At 2:00pm, the divisional police stormed into the university gate with three armoured vehicles. Right from the gate, they released teargases and countless shootings in the air. As soon as the students saw them, they became tense. The campus became chaotic as everyone took to their heels haphazardly.

'See! See! Police with guns and teargases!' some students screamed.

The protesters ran for shelter, scattering into different directions. In the bid to outrun one another into safety, some students collided with each other. Some fell to the tarmac ground and were stepped on.

Also, two asthmatic students were reported to have died as they inhaled the gasses released by the police. The environment was filled with much irritation.

Chinwe and Cynthia stayed indoors. They neither went out nor participated in the violent act. Chinwe peeped through the window again and saw a countless number of students running and jamming their doors.

This is outrageous - from twenty- five thousand naira to fifty thousand! No! It can't be. Why? What do they expect the students to do? How do they expect students to raise that amount? A multitude of questions sprinted through her head. There were no answers- yes, no answers to them. She looked at Cynthia.

'Hmmm! You didn't take part in the protest; you just decided to return, why?' Chinwe teased sonorously, looking expectant.

'You must be joking! You don't know what you're saying. How can I take part in such kind of protest? So you want me dead- I still want to live o. Right now, the thought of what to do rings in me. See dear, we can't stay in this campus today, we can't even spend a night here, it's unhealthy,' Cynthia said.

Chinwe sighed. 'But why the sudden increase in the fees at this critical time in the country? They didn't just increase it but they doubled the fee...'

'Well,' said Cynthia, interrupting Chinwe.

> *Don't mind our uncaring government.*
> *Behold them sitting in cat bird seats*
> *Behold them doctoring papers with*
> *inks and pens.*
> *Behold them making policies*
> *favourable to them,*
> *Behold them making the seats of*
> *government an*
> *Ancestral stool; 'leaders of tomorrow'*
> *They called the youths. From my*
> *Birth have I heard that cliché.*
> *How can the youths lead when even*
> *with*
> *Grey hairs they strive anxiously for*
> *power?*
> *Behold them, claiming they are*
> *building the*
> *Country, through their looting and*
> *Exploitation?*
> *They have destroyed this home*
> *Yet they claim to build. When the*
> *Foundation is ruptured*
> *Aren't the builders building in vain?*
> *They do not even consider the poor*
> *That brought them to power.*
> *The masses are suffering.*
> *In a time like this, a time when the*

Country is in a great puzzle, the
students'
Fee is increased at a double rate.
All the youths can do is to keep praying
For change and transformation in
This country's leaders of tomorrow
indeed!' Cynthia yelled.

Chinwe watched her speak with serious attention.

'We have to leave this campus!' said Cynthia.

'I don't want to go to the village now! Where are we leaving to?' Chinwe asked.

'Alright, we can go to my Uncle's house in the city, we can stay there until the campus is fully back to normal. There may be suspension of activities for now,' Cynthia replied. They threw few of their clothes and shoes into a bag. Cynthia quickly picked her phone and dialed her uncle's mobile. She told him she was coming home with her friend. They returned to the campus after one week when things were calm and stable. This happened in their final year.

CHAPTER NINE

It was morning in Umuozo. Maazi Udoka and Mma had risen so early. The cock crowed as the bright day gradually unfolded just like a newly hatched chicken which peeping out from a fresh egg's broken shell. It was cold at this season, the weak lights slowly filtered into the village houses.

The people of the village had risen to their daily routine of toiling and hard labour. They were known to be busy. It was a farming season; the rain had come to make the farms bloom. The yam foliage enjoyed more gaps at the farms in darkened colours and the maize leaves had changed their colours too. There were lots of activities by everyone in the village but the land had been corked up in quietude like a grave yard! Everyone had deserted it, the farmers had all gone to the farms as they were now reassured in their farming activities. They all now worked with will. The traders in the land too had all gone to the market to make ends meet.

For the family of Maazi Udoka, today would be an important day. Chinwe would come home with a stranger- a visitor, to introduce as her soul mate.

Chinwe had graduated from the university after four years of studies. She had also completed a one-year National Youth Service at Asaba where she taught commerce in a Government secondary school.

She had met many suitors prior to the completion of her youth service. Their offers of marriage were like a heap of cassava tubers at the end of a feast. Her chilled mind was neither caused to stir nor beat for any of the men. At the tenth month she was caught. She was caught like a fish hooked out of water with a fisher's baited hook. She met frank. Captivated was she by his mien.

Frank was a light skinned young man who was tall and slim. He had that look which titillated the heart and soothed the eyes. Chinwe appreciated all she saw in him the moment she set her eyes on him- *love at first sight*. Yes it was *love* she felt. He graduated as an engineer from one of the Western prestigious universities. Frank worked with an engineering company in the Eyimba city. He had met Chinwe in a bus on his way to his friend's wedding at Asaba.

Inside the bus, frank sat by Chinwe's side. They had only exchanged greetings and after that there was no discussion between them. Frank felt attracted to her. He was thrilled at what he saw. A perfect girl.

Everything about her was charming. But it was a first sight attraction. How could he conclude about who she truly was? His mind resolved with an air of ease. Her manners and carriage were pleasant from what he saw. Everything was perfect in his eyes!

Frank constituently did everything possible to make her notice him. Within him, he thought of several tricks and hints to win her heart. Just at first sight, Chinwe discovered his constant stare at her. She pretended however. She proved careless to his look. Yes. She was to display coyness as morality demanded for it- A coy attitude. She became conscious of herself but in her heart was a special likeness for him. She was drooling over him already. It was truly *love at first sight.* But it was said that love is developed through a relationship; one does not love whom they do not know. Can one just fall in love at first sight? The society considers it evil for a woman to be the one wooing a man. Even when the woman is stoically dying in love for a man, she would wait for the man to approach her first and when he does, morality demands that she hesitates at first. But why should this be the norm? Who made this social norm? Chinwe thought silently.

The bus journeyed for some minutes before they alighted and rank finally mustered courage to talk to her. They had been quiet all this while but prior to the bus stop, he broke the silence. 'Hi beautiful lady. I'm Frank. You have been tongue-tied all this while,' She feigned absent mindedness.

Was her mind inside the vehicle? What could she be thinking? Nothing, her mind was there. 'Speak to me dear,' Frank tapped her now. 'What's the problem? Your mind has really gone far. Far. Far. Far has it gone...to where?' he teased.

The discussion grew to its peak. They introduced themselves. Though she had imbued that syndrome of, *I don't give my name and data to strangers*, she finally succumbed to the introduction. Yes. Not after all the sweet words that spilled out of his mouth. His mouth was as sweet as honey- if not sweeter. As his sweet words fell into her ears, she was cold. As cold as ice. He requested for her mobile number which she gave to him after a feigned hesitation. She must imbibe the rules of decency; the rules of morality; *the hard to get syndrome.*

Frank called her subsequently. He had remembered often what he learned from a particular seminar he attended which was called: *'Seminar for singles and married'.* His mind had always flashed to the teachings of the male speaker. He had often ruminated on the ideas the seminar gave.

'Don't expect to win her heart in a matter of days. Slow but steady wins the race.

Set realistic expectations so that you will not be disappointed if she does not fall for you immediately...' Frank recalled.

He remembered all the steps he was taught on how to make her fall for him. He made enough effort to win her; he constantly visited Asaba from the city of Eyimba. He became so conscious of himself. He became more coordinated. He packaged himself well. His dressing changed like that of one engaged in a dress rehearsal in order to appear in a more gorgeous look. He remembered that the seminar's speaker had also said to them; *'Look your best. You may not care how much you look like but women definitely do. It's not so much the clothes and the hygiene that is important. It's the message you send to the rest of the world- that you take care of yourself; that you know your style, and that you're confident.'*

He patiently applied all the principles of relationship which he learned and at the end he succeeded in wooing her though she had proved *'hard to get'*. The relationship grew vastly to its peak and they agreed to get married. Their plans for marriage went on blithely between them. Chinwe and frank had looked forward to their wedding day with the expectant excitement of a child longing for Christmas.

***

Mma had risen at the prime of time- a time when the sun invited itself fully into the day without being called. She had set her kitchen in order. Her husband had caught a game during evening before the stated day. She had her cauldron steaming steeply in profusion with meat. She had prepared a sumptuous meal to be taken in gusto. She left the meal smouldering in the glowing cooker.

They waited anxiously for Chinwe and her visitor. Mma was huddled with the thought of her arrival. 'What could be keeping them this long? It's almost noon and they aren't here yet.' she said.

'Oh you worry a lot! Don't worry yourself too much. They'll be here soon, very soon. It's a distance from Asaba to this place. The thirsty fig sits waiting patiently, waiting for the arrival of the rains,' Maazi Udoka shrugged.

Chinwe finally arrived with frank - her fiancée; their visit hit the right note. Things had really worked out just as Chinwe expected. Frank was really entertained by his prospective in- laws. Hospitality was a virtue to Mma. No guest left her home without a burning flame of felicity by her treatment. Frank introduced himself to the family after which he left with glee.

Chinwe was drenched with brimming torrents of happiness. She danced like a snake and smiled like a burnt goat with teeth flashing out white. In her mind was the abode of joy. Her family had unanimously accepted frank with open arms. She had thought of being harangued especially by her mother. Her fear had been that the parents may speak against her marriage inclination to frank who was from Anambra. Her mother had always told her that she preferred a woman especially an *Ada*, getting married to a man from her parent's side. But the reverse had been the case here. There was no grudge on that. Not an atom of it.

In her frenzied state, she chuckled. She discovered the house clean and tidy, the floor scrubbed and the murky waters around the compound were drained. The broken windows were also amended. *Mama will never cease to amaze me*, she thought.

She swelled round the compound with mirth. There was nothing bashful in the home. Not a single thing. Who might have done all these? Indeed, a home is where the heart is. She frolicked and danced like a little girl at frank's departure.

'Mama, you shouldn't have spent so much time cleaning the house,' she said 'you're such a loving mother…'

Mma interrupted. 'It was your brother. How could I have done all these at my age? Your brother came home early to tidy up the house. Have you seen him? He even hurt his hand while amending the broken window,'

'*Chimuo!* My God! Where is he?' she screeched.

She rashly headed to Obinna's room in fast steps. On seeing his pale thin face, she felt pricked in her heart. Pricked with hundreds of needles. 'Just because of me? Why? Why should you do all these for me?' she asked. He looked at her with a hush. After few minutes, his face released a smile of profuse happiness. His tongue let go of words after his silence.

'I'm not complaining dear,' Obinna said.

'Why should you? Why?'

'There is no elephant that complains about the weight of its trunk. No elephant is burdened by the weight of its sizes,' he answered.

Chinwe was dampened into silence. She couldn't speak. Could there by anyone like him on earth? No, there was none to compare to Obinna. He is all in all.

She quickly made to her bag, brought out a therapeutic ointment and applied it to his wound. She bandaged it afterwards.

'*Obim*, does it hurt?' she asked.

'*Mba*, it doesn't . . . I feel no pain,'

'I know it hurts you...you shouldn't have done this.'

'What pain can be compared to that which I get at the construction site? Even at the injuries from the falling stones and bricks, I never ceased my duties. I keep working, this is just a mere injury!' he replied.

'Okay dear, you'll be fine. *Ndo,*' Chinwe said and caressed his bushy head filled with unshaved hairs.

'Yes. I must be fine,' Obinna smiled. He continued, 'I couldn't join in when he came. How was it? And how is he?'

'It really went well dear. He's fine too. He has left. I didn't know you were around. I would have called you to join us. Papa later told me he didn't want to disturb you since you already have an injury,'

'That's nothing dear. This was just his first coming. He would come again and again- several comings before the main event. I would get to meet him soon- very soon,'

'Yes, he will surely visit soon. You're such a loving brother. What can I do without you?'

'It's okay. I've really missed you. Thank God you've found happiness in him. All good things come to those who wait.'

'I love you.' Chinwe said and remained silent. None could break the prevailing silence. It was still- very still, as still as untroubled water. As still as death.

In the middle of the deadened state, Chinwe turned back on Obinna. At a wink of an eye, there were tears flowing from her cloudily brimmed eyes, down to her face.

At this time, Chinwe was 26 years old and Obinna was 23 years old.

CHAPTER TEN

The darkest hour is just before dawn.

Chinwe stood in her husband's house in reminiscence. After a year, she had been married and wedded to Frank. The search for happiness had been as smooth as she hoped. With her brother, life had been fair to her; he had been her solace at all times of her life. He was her everything, could she have been at her present stage without him?

She had moved into Frank's house at Faulks road, Aba, Eyimba city. She had also snugged there like a bug in a rug. She had been a bundle of radiance. Her wedding with Frank was a big show and it had been the talk of the town; just as she anticipated. It heated the city.

Her spirits grew higher and higher and she was not at all negligent of this. Her mind was unbent. And she had found a predilection in her unbent mind. She knew there was a flowing felicity in her like a tranquil runnel.

She had always stayed chirpy. Life was indeed moving at the right pace. All the strata of her life were as she had counted upon. As she regurgitated her ecstatic moments, her mind sparkled in intoxication. Yes, her brother had paid a high price to make her life a zest. *You must go to school to be empowered-* he had often said to her. Tell me, where is it written that a man must be greater than a woman? Tell me, who said a woman shouldn't excel more than a man?

She soliloquized:

With him was the track of
Life drawn for me.
With him were my legs
Set for the run
With my ears attentive to it.
With him was my oil of strength.
Poured in sprightliness for this
Race of life.
With him is the trophy won.
From one stage to another
The map he held led me through.
The burning picture of my future now
In reality, as expected
Now is my bond in matrimony.
Like a yam tendril has my life grown
To its vast; all with him!

She was at home alone so she moved in a surge inside her room. Frank had gone to his office. He had been made the director of the factory where he worked. Countless times Chinwe and Frank had bid Maazi Udoka and his wife, Mma, to come and live with them in the city. They had always objected.

Maazi Udoka had kept mum the thought that it was not possible for him to lay bed in his son-in-law's house with his wife. What would people say? That he was not capable of manning his home? Besides, what would the young man's parents say? That would be unfair. A man does not run away from his home into another man's home. These and other thoughts spouted his mind.

'A tree is known by its fruit. You have proved to be good children. We would love to come and live with you in the city but you see, we can't leave our house empty in this village to come to the city. Besides, if we leave the village, we wouldn't know what to do there. But don't worry dear, when things are fully matured – when the God of fruitfulness blesses your marriage- when you give birth, your mother would come for the *Umugo* –child visit.' Maazi Udoka had said to Chinwe and Frank.

Obinna had concurred with his father's opinion. He said to Chinwe, 'Sister, don't worry about papa and mama. *Biko*, just take care of your own parents-in-law. I would take good care of them here, *inugo*.'

Obinna had also turned down an offer. He had refused to accept being the manager of maintenance department at Frank's engineering company. As the director of the company, Frank had offered Obinna the opportunity to be the manager of maintenance. Chinwe had worked it out with her husband – as little indemnification and requital for his sacrifices for her. Nothing can be done to equate his benevolence, she thought. Obinna had only insisted on working as a repair man instead, at least for the main time.

***

In her solitude, her mind glinted with joy. Sadness was varnished from her exultant mind- not even an exiguous one was found present in her. She plodded the room and found a newspaper which Frank brought from the vendor while returning from office in the evening the day before.

Chinwe took the papers. Reading had become her hobby- especially newspapers. She had cultivated this habit during her university days with her friend, Cynthia. Cynthia had facilitated her newspaper reading habit; she had planted and watered it; now it had grown into a large tree of reading readiness. She had made her believe that papers were more genuine and could be referenced when it comes to the latest happenings in the society. She now preferred reading hard copy papers to the soft copy on the internet. She seldom watched television or listened to radio for news.

She wobbly took the papers, turned to the front page and the headline fascinated her. 'Oh my God! *Tufiakwa!*' she exclaimed.

'Could this be true?' she added. At this moment, alternating currents of reading readiness crowded her anxious mind. She sat down quickly, flipped through the pages, and dictated the story's page. With rapt attention, she read the headline loudly:

Revealed: Baby Factory in the State

'It was reported that a woman owned a baby factory in the state where she bought and sold babies to interested buyers in exchange of huge amounts of money. It was said that she bought a baby boy at the amount of one hundred thousand naira and often sold it at the price of four hundred and fifty thousand naira. On the other hand, she bought a baby girl at the price of eighty thousand naira and sold at four hundred thousand naira. This was as a result of the so much interest and admiration attached to the male child by the society.'

Yes, the society attached so much importance to male children and this was why it cost so much to have a male. Even in matrimonial home, women strived to have male children as fulfillment of their marriages. Chinwe thought intensively. But why? Why should so much importance be attached to male children at the detriment of females? Her mind recalled a certain situation in her village, Umuozu, where some daughters were disinherited from their family land. Why? Simply because there was no male among them? Could it be because those daughters were not empowered? Maybe lack of enlightenment kept them in the dark. They couldn't assert their rights. Educational empowerment enlightens women and liberates them from social hegemony.

Chinwe had her mind boiling with thoughts. Why are women often made to feel inadequate? Why is a woman subjected to mental and social torture because she has no male child? Why? Why? Her soul asked a multitude of questions. She concluded within her – injustice to the female folk. Yes, injustice in the highest order. Macho chauvinism! Equity must be given to both gender- male and female. Aren't children inheritance from the Lord? Yes, the fruit of the womb, His reward. She remembered the bible passage. In her hitting mind, she resolved: if the society begins to consider striking a balance on the worth of children; regardless of the gender, then harmony would rest in the hearts of all. With social empowerment, this can be achieved.

Chinwe was struck when she read that the buyers of the children resided in a nearby village to Umuozo, her home town. They bought these babies for different reasons. Some officials of the Nigerian Security and Civil Defense Corps (NSCD) were said to have busted the baby factory some days ago.

The paper reported that the police arrested the owner of the factory as well as her two accomplices. They had also rescued thirty-two pregnant teenagers. The rescued teenagers were reported to be girls kicked out of their homes by their parents after becoming pregnant at their fresh ages due to pre-marital sex affairs.

Kicking the girls out of their homes, was it the right thing done by parents? Chinwe thought. Kicked out of home, they were accepted into the factory by the owner who took care of them for the entire pregnancy period. These parents had only succeeded in pushing out their girls to the streets- to become street women. They become women of easy virtues. Each time they gave birth, they sold their babies to the proprietor of the factory. It was also said that the girls who were interested in earning more money could stay in the factory. They often stayed to be impregnated by men who paid to the proprietor to have them as sex mates and after which they would sell their babies again.

Chinwe continued her thoughts. She showered countless blames on the parents of such girls. As humans, she mulled, the parents ought to experience a wide range of emotions, from shock and disappointment to grief and worry about the future- the future of their daughters and the family name. Some also feel a great deal of guilt, thinking that if only they'd done more to protect their girls this wouldn't have occurred. It is indeed likely to be a difficult time for the family irrespective of the feelings they're experiencing. But parents should know that their children- teens especially, need them more than ever. Yes. Being able to communicate with each other- especially when emotion is running high- is essential. Teens that carry a baby to full term have special health concerns and they would have a healthier pregnancy- emotionally and physically- if they truly know that their parents are there for them regardless.

Chinwe had this resolution within her. To her, parents are to recognize their feelings and work through them so that they can accept and support their pregnant teen. Does it mean they don't have the right to feel disappointed and even angry? No. such reactions are common. But they must get beyond their initial feelings for the sake of their own pregnant child.

The NSCDC director Mr. kingsly Okorie added that the baby factory was officially registered with the government but its owner's real business was illegal, thus the owner must be made to face the law.

Chinwe couldn't believe it when she read that the owner of the baby factory was said to be a police officer's wife, Mrs. Nneoma Mbakwe, the wife of Mr. Chigbo Mbakwe.

'Our madam (Mrs. Mbakwe) is unlawfully arrested. She is not guilty. She's only aiding couples from Lagos, Abuja, Port Harcourt, Calabar and other Places by selling male and female babies at an agreed fee. She also settles the mothers of the babies and takes her profit as balance,' said a short, black young woman.

Another younger woman in her late teens added; 'Our madam would soon be released,' This younger woman has a protruding stomach that seemed almost due for delivery. She was later identified as Nkeiruka. She had stayed at the baby factory for three years. Her parents had disowned her- she was impregnated at the age of sixteen and couldn't track the man who was responsible for her plight. She had several affairs so it was difficult for her to identify who the father of her child was. That was when she was still in senior secondary school, class two. Her parents had sent her away to search for the father of her unborn child. Nkeiruka had left and had run into the baby factory. Since then, she had had three more children.

'This is not the first time she is been detained. They would release her soon. Why are the security men here? Visitors are not allowed into this building except for clients who come for business or teenage girls who desire to sell their babies to prospective buyers,' explained one of the factory girls by the name Halima. Halima is a Hausa girl from the northern part of the country. Her father is a famous *Alhaji* who sells onions in bags at Cemetery market in the Eyimba city-a dealer in onions. An Igbo trader had planted a seed into her and had denied her. The fear of her fanatic father made her to stray from home. She wouldn't like to be ill-treated by her father who had often told her and her siblings never to have any serious thing to do with Igbos whom they called *'Nyamiri'*. He had also cautioned her strictly when he discovered she had been meeting countless Nyamiri *guys.* So, the factory gave her a home in the absence of her home. But to each of the young women there, the factory equipped them with better skills needed for prostitution. It certificated them into *the world of easy virtue.*

Chinwe read the story to the end with rapt attention. She was so much engrossed in her reading. 'Wonders will never cease to end in this country. Bad news travel so fast. Each day carries its own.' she said.

She opened the next page, in it was a story; *Six paraded for kidnapping in Ebonyi*

She skimmed through the story and her mind was filled with consternation for what? The events happening around the country!

Her phone rang conspicuously now. She watched the phone vibrating beside her on the sofa. She hissed, who could it be? Was she expecting any important call? Anyway, anyone could call. It could be family or even friends. *The one who calls you is the one who loves and cares for you,* she thought. The phone rang and rang again, dancing ceaselessly on the sofa. It was Cynthia her friend, calling after a very long time. Has she called to give 'the date'? She cogitated. She picked the call and laughed heartily.

'Hello! Hello!' Chinwe said, elated.

'Madam Chinwe! How are doing?' Cynthia asked.

'We're fine dear. You've not be fair to us. It's been a while since you called,' Chinwe said. 'Even when I tried calling, your numbers were unavailable. Frank himself seems to be worried about you. He has asked after you more than a thousand times!'

Cynthia laughed heavily. 'My dear you will not understand. I've been so busy, very busy. Can I say as busy as a bee?' She paused, grinning. 'Life as a journalist and reporter has been piled up with lots of frantic activities, traveling here and there. It's not easy dear!'

'Really? That's the spirit! Life of an empowered woman,'

'Chinwe! You and this empowerment thing!'

'You sound so happy Cynthia, I've been expecting lots of good news from you. When will you name the date? You told me you were hooked up to one banker. Your voice sounds like that of one clouded with good news. Have you called to give the date? Has...'

Cynthia interrupted. 'Hmmm! *Nne, nwere ya nwayo* ! Take it easy. Am I not the one who called? You're running so fast, it is little by little that a bird builds its nest. I've good news for you but you mustn't forget that one does not become a master diviner in a day. A forest is not made in a season. The swoop of an eagle has seen many seasons and floods,' The two friends burst out into laughter.

'Chi, the last time I called, I told you l was employed as a T.V Reporter at the National Television Station in Calabar. This time around, the date has been fixed. I know that's the only thing you would like to hear. I can see your itching ears,'

'Really? That's the good news I want to hear. An empowered woman! Now you're talking...'

'So I have not been talking before? Okay. I shall be tying the knot with him in the next four weeks. I want you and Frank to storm Calabar for my wedding, you must be there!'

'Yes! That's what I've been waiting to hear. I guess he's the banker, isn't he?' Chinwe asked enthusiastically.

'Oh! Chinwe you are too curious. So you haven't changed. Frank hasn't changed your curiosity. Okay, since you want to know, I shall be tying the knot with a young, handsome lecturer,'

Chinwe interrupted. 'Lecturer *kwa*! Cyndi baby, tell me more about it, how did you get the catch?'

Cynthia laughed and continued. 'He lectures at University of Calabar's English department. His name is Emeka Nwafor and he is from Imo state. You know what? I've fallen head over heels for him,'

'What about the banker?' Chinwe asked.

'That one?' Cynthia giggled. 'That one minute man; I detest him. He's so damn weak- too weak for my liking,'

Chinwe smiled broadly. 'Really? You mean he's weak in the bedroom business. Why don't you help him?'

'Haven't I tried enough? He's just too weak; he doesn't exceed his one minute job. I think he's just complacent with his ability and I'm not. The most irritating is his refusal to take supplements that could boost his energy. Like you know, no woman needs a man like him- a weakling,' Cynthia snapped out with military precision.

'True dear, no woman needs a man as such. Every woman needs love. Every woman needs a caring man. By care, the bedroom business is never excluded .One minute men will go nowhere,' Chinwe snorted.

'Dear, you see, I can't be tied to someone who doesn't have time for himself let alone, me. These bankers are too chocked up with their duties and activities. I think stress turns some of them into one minute entities,' Cynthia said, bearing in mind that this one minute experience does not apply to all bankers. She detested stereotypes. She needed to be careful of her use of language. She knew very well that the beauty of language lied in the elegance of its meaning. But was it stress or activities that reduced the strength of men like that?

Maybe, she concluded, bearing in mind that all men cannot be the same. She continued with the conversion. 'A woman needs love. She needs one who has enough time for her; not one who would be so busy with activities and ends up in the bedroom doing a minute business. Come to think of it, who will take care of our kids when we are married? As a journalist, I have a lot on my plate and he is a banker who has a lot on his plate too. While we were dating, he hardly even squeezed out time for me. Dear, I thought of all these and when Emeka showed up, I found in him a better husband! Do you also know the best of it?'

'No! Tell me!'

'Emeka doesn't have a mother. His mother is long dead. So I won't have any wicked mother-in-law to contend with. Most of these mothers are witches who will not allow their daughter-in-laws to rest and enjoy their marriages. They constitute high blood pressure to the ladies. I've always told you that I'll never marry a man whose mother is still alive. So Emeka is the deal. The guy is so hot!'

'Really? I see he gives it to you real hard,' she smiled. 'So because Emeka, the lecturer showed up you gave the banker a red card?'

'Why shouldn't I? Chinwe, I can't just take it. The mother-in-law issue too. I can't take rubbish from any mother-in-law who will like to lord over me!'

'Some mother-in-laws could be challenging. But will you like to be dead before your son marries a wife?' Chinwe paused. She expected an answer to this question but the answer she awaited didn't come. She continued. 'Anyway, it's not easy being with some mothers. You've always said it that any man whose mother is alive shouldn't cross your way. And any *obodo oyibo* man as well.' They both laughed uncontrollably. 'Tell me, how did it happen between you and this your Emeka? Remember I told you how it happened between Frank and me? So tell me the story. Tell me all about it!'

'*Onye ashiri!* Enough of my explanations; when I come, I shall tell you everything you need to hear. Hope you and Frank will be home during the weekend?' Cynthia asked.

'Yes we shall be waiting for you,' replied Chinwe.

'I shall come to give you the invitation card. Also, you shall accompany me for shopping in Aba,'

'*Wao!* I'm so happy for you dear, congratulations!'

'Thank you Chinwe, I would be expecting good news of a happy event from you soon. Bye for now, till we see,' said Cynthia.

'Bye! I can't wait to see you and your Emeka. I can't even wait to come for the wedding. We shall be excepting you,' Chinwe said. She laughed warmly as the call ended.

In the dark

CHAPTER ELEVEN

The day's morning was different from the other mornings of the season. It had been summoned into the city after a cloudy and misty midnight which later resulted in a torrential burst from the wailing sky.

The sun steeply welcomed itself into the day. It had come out lazily like a lobster. The trees had blotted it out with their branches and leaves. But how long could this be?

Gradually, as the day unfurled, the sun manoeuvred the day's activities. It peeped through the eyes of leaves to scorch the humans fiercely with its wings of light. It also forcibly opened the earth's mouth to swallow the murky waters of the night. With its presence, the day was mellowed for human animation and enterprises.

✻✻✻

It was an unpleasant day for Obinna. However, Obinna thanked God a million times. His life was saved. He didn't lose his life. What could they have done? And what would people have said? People would speak and give several fabricated stories about his death. That's if he had died.

He now worked at the factory with Frank. He had chosen to work as a repair man in charge of electrical appliances instead of a maintenance manager. As a maintenance manager, he was to lead, coach and empower the workers in a positive manner to maximize their potentials and their contributions to key performance goals for the company. He was to supervise the installing and maintenance of all machine tools and related equipment. Also, he was to solve the problems in hydraulic, pneumatic, and mechanical system. He was not to involve in any form of repairs but to stay in the office and be in control of maintenance. Despite the relative ease that came with being a maintenance manager, Obinna opted to be a repairman.

Since Obinna had chosen to be a repairman, he was given two weeks intensive training by Mr. Effiong Ossai; a chocolate-skinned man from Akwa Ibom. Mr Effiong seemed like a man in his early fifties. He had thick lips and a wrinkled round face. He was short and hardly smiled; even when he forced a smile, his smile and frown were no different from each other.

Surprisingly, as old as he looked, Mr. Effiong was actually in his early thirties. He was the company's trainer in charge of training new staff members. Obinna's duties as a repairman included the repair or replacement of defective equipment parts, using hand tools and power tools. He was to clean or lubricate shafts, bearings, gears or other parts of machinery. He was to also be in charge of electrical appliances which included wiring. Mr. Effiong had given him a thorough and uncompromising training.

That morning, Obinna worked on a cable connected to a high pole inside the factory. He climbed a ladder while repairing the cable which had in it, a life flowing current. He never knew the current was flowing- flowing like an undisturbed stream. His hand touched the naked wire and he got electrocuted. It was a pernicious electrocution but his skin was resistant to the total flow of the current which impeded it from circulating to his heart or brain. His body jerked and jerked on the ladder and he fell down conspicuously from the ladder. Alerted, he was rescued by four of his colleagues who were at the scene of the event. They had grabbed him from falling to the ground with so much surveillance. Immediately, he was rushed to a private clinic at St. Michael road. Had he fallen to the ground, he would have sustained a broken spine. Wouldn't that have been the worst?

Bad news travel fast.

Frank and Chinwe had visited Obinna at the hospital. Chinwe was so tensed. She craved to have her way into his ward. In her mind was a growing turbulent of nervousness. She thought of what to do and thousands of blames for him plunged out of her mind. If he had accepted the position of a maintenance manager, would this have occurred to him? He was placed in a better position, but he chose to suffer. Why? What does he find pleasing in such a position? She thought.

She moved around him with her eyes grievously fixed on him. She became down in the mouth as she watched the plaster casted on his leg. She grumbled a million times.

'Why? Why did you reject being a Manager? A manager does not engage in hazardous things like that. Now look at what you have put yourself into. You are suffering this serious injury. Why didn't you listen to me?' she upbraided.

Obinna's face changed and his clenched teeth uncovered a smile. With a serious expression on his face, he stoically defended his decision. 'Think about your brother – in-law, he just became the director. What would be said of me if I also become the manager without any qualification? What kind of stories do you think would fly around?

Chinwe was filled with keenness. Her eyes crowded tears in them. 'But you lacked in education only because of me. You sacrificed your life for me!' she sobbed.

'Why do you always talk about the past? Let's roll up the past into the waste bin,' Obinna said as he held her hand.

That year, Obinna was twenty- six years and Chinwe was twenty-nine years.

CHAPTER TWELVE

Chinwe wept. Darkness had made its abode the family of Maazi Udoka and the people of Umuozo had shared from its overwhelming features. The ugly event of the day made a bright day dark.

Her eyes gushed out fulsome tears. Her life was in shambles. Franks had made countless efforts to console and recuperate her from grief. She had stayed recumbent at home for days. Her pillows had been soaked in plenitude of tears. But she must be dwindled to a life of ease. What might have happened?

If the load is too heavy for someone to carry, one would be better off to give the load to the ground to carry.

'You can't cry your life to death. God gives and he takes at His own time. Death is a clarion call which all mortals must succumb to. Do you want to go with him?' Frank said to Chinwe.

'Why must death take him so soon? How can I be a failed woman? He's gone without seeing his grandchildren- I've really failed; failed in making him fulfilled,' Chinwe cried. Her thought of failure in marriage and failure in her own family kindled a burning fire of weeping in her. She made weeping a daily routine for a period of time.

In her muzzy state, her tongue was corked up for some minutes with the wailing drums throbbing in her with strong echoes. She couldn't respond to words. The news about his death had flown into her ears through a phone call. She sniveled:

Nnam! Nnam !
My father! My father!
Now are you gone to dance with
the spirits?
Now have you got a new
habitation where
Your fathers are?
Now have you joined a new
blood bloodied
But unbowed?
Though you have eaten the fruit
of honour
Shall we dig in your feet to let
you go?
Now is your nomenclature
Changed with all titles
Gone with you.
What can we mortals do but to
answer the
call of Death.

✽✽✽

Maazi Udoka had died in the village. He was diagnosed of diabetes at the village health centre. Treatments had been given to him and he soon began to recuperate. However, his body relapsed to a worst state shortly a week after his treatment and this drew him finally to his ancestors in the spirit world – *ala mmuo*.

He was a mogul. Every member of the village, both the low and mighty sought for him. He was known to be a benefactor to those who ran to him for aid; he withheld nothing from them. His arms were opened to receive anyone with ease. Thus, his benevolence made people to come to his aid any time he sought for one as *one good turn deserves another*. To him, religious activities were an afterthought. He attended the Roman Catholic Church at seldom. One could count the three seasons of his church attendance; the New Year day- *afo ohuru*, Easter day and Christmas day. His death meant nothing to the church as his visits were countable ones. Also, he neither paid dues nor his tithes. Just a year before his death, he was made a chief and a member of the *Igwe's* cabinet as a result of his wisdom and tolerance.

The people of Umuozo made his death a highly ritualized event. They had it filled with deep mourning. As a chief, his traditional burial rites involved two funerals in order to safely escort him from the realm of the living to *Alammuo*- the spirit world. After the funerals, the deceased would pass from the time of '*ita okazi*' – a period of torment into repose.

His compound bubbled with lots of activities from the members of *Amaala* who trooped in and out to make the gathering a convivial one. Men of two legs and three legs had gathered in the compound. The *Umuadas*- female age group sat around Mma like an aged woman surrounded by grandchildren. The youths went into the *obi* forming a semi-circle.

They had started singing their songs of sorrow. Ulumma- an aged woman whose body shivered as she walked led the songs. Her teeth were coloured from kola nut stains. She chanted dirges sonorously. People said that was her specialty; she was well known in the village. Her songs were said to go deeply into the land of the spirits. But could her songs wake the death to rise? Weren't they made to soften the rock-like hearts of the living? The songs reminded all that death is a red cap which must be worn by all. This cap fits anyone unquestionably, but at a particular time.

Mazi Udoka's burial was to be done in accordance to custom and tradition of the land, with no interference from the church. He was not a member but a mere visitor. As a chief, the deceased body was not taken to the mortuary. It was also not subjected to any post- mortem. The rules of traditional burials had been strictly adhered to; the elders had spelt out the stipulated rules to his son- Obinna.

Obinna had really grown to his responsibilities as the first and only son of the family. On his shoulders lied the duty to give his father a befitting funeral. Could he bear this alone? What affects the nose must also affect the eyes that must weep for it.

Frank and the other members of the clan had assured Obinna of their endless backup. The extended family members had also divided the funeral's purposed amount amongst themselves in order to make it grand. All arrangements had been made for the day.

***

There had been a wake keep which lasted the whole night at the bereaved compound. Gun shots were fired to alert the villagers about the death. The body was interred after the wake keep in a grave dug inside the deceased's compound.

Prior to the burial were certain preparations. The corpse was stretched out on plantain leaves, sponged down thoroughly, and rubbed with cam wood dye to mark it as sacred. These preparations were done to cleanse the body. After all these, the cadaver was laid out in the living room. It was lied down with its feet facing the entry way.

After these necessary preparations, it was believed that the body had been made set for free passage from the world of the living to the spirit world- *ala mmuo*.

As the heir, Obinna had welcomed the members of the community, and the invited guests into the bereaved family with kola nuts and palm wine. Prayers and libations were also offered to summon the ancestral spirits into the home to escort the spirit of the deceased. This was the first burial.

Mma, the wife of the deceased, couldn't believe her husband had gone into silence. She wailed pathetically. Her husband had gone and must be buried like the others. Could this be my husband? She thought within her, with her lips grasping and her feet shivering in agony.

Clothed in black, she ran towards the grave weeping and shouting. 'I must be interred with him! Death is so cruel to leave me lonely. I'm painted in the corner,' she continued, 'what is left of me? Take me too you wicked monster, my soul now thirsts to be relocated by you into his new abode now that you have made him feckless, motionless and silent in this place of worms.'

She spread herself on the grave. She lied facing the blue sky, with her hands raising the sands of the grave. She saturated herself with the sand. 'Let me die now!' she screamed.

'Stop her! Stop her! Take her in!' shouted the eldest man around, Maazi Okwudiri. He was a dark and huge man with a pot-like belly. He had grey hairs all over his head and beards and a flat nose on his swollen face that haboured two tribal marks.

Mma was grabbed and tightly held by the *Umuada*. She was taken into her cottage, a small house where she stayed with her mourners.

After a day, the second burial was held. It was meant to complete the funeral rites. This time around, it was accompanied by feasting and merry- making rather than mourning. The bereaved family and their visitors had appeared in colourful attires. The scene had been marked with singing and traditional dances by all. It was also like an eating competition where all the village gluttons where assembled into eating. Food was provided with lots of drinks for the people whose numbers were like the countless sands of a sea shore. There were displays of different masquerades. The frightening gun shots of different canons were heard. The family spent lavishly on the burial. One may imagine if the family would go bankrupted after the extravagant spending.

Seven moons after the interment and rituals, Obinna had a dream. In his dream, he saw his father in a happy mood, dancing with his ancestors.

The spot was gloomy as the sun had receded to welcome the full moon and stars to kiss the cosmic into darkness. The dance of the spirits as he saw was at the shrine of the ancestors, at the heart of the night- the very heart of darkness. The gods, goddesses, and ancestors had all assembled as they dined together in gusto to welcome Maazi Udoka into his permanent home.

Obinna saw all the ancestors and *arishis* present as they were present at their convivial celebration. He was able to recognize his late grandfather- Uloko, the late Igwe- Eze Adindu and the late Nwokoro, a member of the *Igwe*'s cabinent. The spirits sang as they danced hilariously.

Dance one, dance all!
Dance for he's finally home
Dance and sound the trumpet
Dance for a gleeful celebration

Dance and play the Ikoro drum,
Drum with your thunderous voices
Flow down the waters in music,
Make them productive in yield.
Chew the kola, jive in gyration
Dance to the tune of music for the mortals
Have made his coming a feast for us
We shall dance!
We shall celebrate!
We shall placate their loss with the birth of a
new soul!

This dream was also confirmed by another member of the extended family; Maazi Okwudiri. The dream signified the deceased repose into the land of the spirits- *ala mmuo*, as interpreted by the tradition.

CHAPTER THIRTEEN

Eighteen months had passed after the burial of late Maazi Udoka.

The family had gradually recuperated from grief. What grief?

Loss.

They had passed through the process of mourning – *Igbankpe* and had also striped-off their sack clothes known as '*akwa nkpe*'.

For the members of the extended family, things were back to normal since all the rituals had been completed. But Mma had something within her. It was the scar of loss; the scar was still in her... Her spirit. Her soul. Her body. It was stamped on her– it was her husband who died; her bone and her flesh. Could this thought ever be washed away from her unstable mind?

✳✳✳

At twenty nine, Obinna had received several pestering for marriage from his family members. There had been a family meeting were all the members of the extended family urged him to get married. Maazi Okwudiri, the eldest, had adjured the members of the family to aid Obinna in *Inu Nwunye* (marriage). It was a general belief that marriage was an indispensable factor for the continuation of a family line.

'Obi, it is time for you to marry in order to beget your own children- to get a family like your parents,' Maazi Okwudiri said during one of those family meetings.

Mma, his mother, had at several times urged him to marry so that she could carry her own grandchildren before death came. She had been requesting for this every morning and during the annual festival while giving cult to her *Chi*. She had been restless especially towards Chinwe – her daughter who had been married without a child. That was the norm. How can a mother be relaxed when her daughter found no fulfillment in matrimony? Resting was a thing of shame. Of what reason could she be living? Didn't her mother do the same for her? On her part, she had sought for solutions to her daughter's childlessness. One could say that she felt the pains more than her daughter. She had even paid visits- uncountable visits to spiritualists on her daughter's behalf. The last spiritualist- *'prophet Oku nagba ozara'* as he was called, was said to be acting in a *churchy* way *known as 'mmiri doritido'*. Mma had been required to make a cleansing sacrifice for Chinwe in order to placate the ancestral spirit of their clan. She had gone to a mountain top with lots of items- two white rams, a yard of white cotton material, a doll, and a huge amount of money. He had assured her that Chinwe would have a set of triplets-two boys and a girl after the ritual. Mma had been mirthful about this. She was on the verge to put her enemies to shame. She had waited and waited. After the waiting- no miracle was seen. It was just like the others. No difference at all. So she had taken it upon herself to pray for her children's wellbeing in marriage.

At thirty years of age, Obinna married someone from the village; a girl named Nwakego (a child out values all money, all wealth). She was the daughter of chief Amadi whose fame sprouted from his yearly prowess of bountiful harvest from farming. Chief Amadi was wealthy and known throughout the community. His wife had been barren for eight years. He was a knight in the village church but he still believed in the power of tradition. His late father had moved from one *dibia* to another with him in the quest for solution to his wife's then barrenness. Finally, after some sacrifices to the goddess of fertility at midnight, she conceived and bore a daughter. The sacrifices were made with a white goat, ten cowries, red and white candles, *fanta*, red oil and a doll. It was done to placate the goddess of fertility. After this, a baby girl was born. She was called 'Nwakego'. The name was courtesy of the long quest for an arrival of a child. Chief Amadi's wife didn't give birth to any other child. He was in no way perturbed by this- he didn't remarry even after several pestering from his kinsmen. He believed in the modern saying that a child is child and human irrespective of the gender. He also said that when an only female child is well groomed, she could serve the duty of a male child. To him, the female gender must never be subjected to any form of mental or social torture because of their sex. They must be free. Justice must be accorded to all; male and female, without prejudice. *All a female child needs is to be empowered*- Chief Amadi believed.

Obinna was eight years older than Nwakego. He had watched her for some months. He had told his mother about her and made his intentions towards her known too. Mma had supported the marriage idea; she claimed to have known Nwakego as a decent girl with an undisputable character. This encouraged Obinna in his journey towards her.

Nwakego answered Obinna in the affirmative two days after his proposal.

Obinna was in a hurry. He wanted her to be his as soon as possible. So after two weeks of Obinna's proposal, Chief Amadi's residence was visited by Obinna and his uncle, Maazi Okwudiri.

Maazi Okwudiri introduced himself and his nephew to Chief Amadi. After this, he hit the hammer on the nail with their marriage proposal.

'Our people said that a toad does not run in the day time for nothing. It must be pursued by something,' Maazi Okwudiri said.

'Yes. It is true. Our people are right. Whatever they said is true,' Chief Amadi smiled.

'I'm here in your house, not alone but here with this young man,'

'Okay. I see,'

'You may know him; he is my late brother's son. His name is Obinna Udoka,'

'My son, welcome to my home,'

Maazi Okwudiri cleared his throat, 'One does not beat around the bush when embarking on a journey.'

'Then you go straight to the point,'

'My son here has seen a very beautiful flower in your compound. He has been restless about it. He would like to pluck it, except if he plucks the flower without permission, he would not be restful. He would forever remain restless. So what do you say?' Maazi Okwudiri said finally with a cracked, heavy voice.

Chief Amadi again welcomed his august visitors and invited his daughter – Nwakego to come. He asked her if she was aware of their coming. She confirmed that she was not unaware. Her confirmation was a pointer to her agreement.

The evening of seven days dwelt in serenity. Obinna was in Chief Amadi's house with concomitant of his uncle and some elders. They brought wine and kola nuts which they presented to the prospective bride's father. In return, they were served sumptuous meals which they all ate and relished.

When they finished eating, the bride price was negotiated among the elders and the bride's father. They only agreed on a symbolic price. But in addition were other prerequisites like kola nuts, palm wines, two goats, chickens, wrappers, yam tubers, drinks and jewelries. It took more than just a sitting before the final bride price was settled upon. The visit also hit a glamorous feast.

Two weeks after, Obinna with his mother, uncle and other elders paid a visit to their in-laws. That evening was meant for the payment of the bride price. Maazi Okwudiri handed the money and the other agreed imperative items over to Chief Amadi. The items were counted as stipulated. The traditional wedding date was fixed just a month ahead. It was to take place at the bride's compound. Everyone present there was served with meal and drinks from the in-laws' kitchen.

***

It was in a month's time; the day fixed for the *Igba nkwu* -wine carrying. The *Igba nkwu* was the climax of marriage according to the Igbo culture. It was the traditional wedding. It brought the *Ikwu na ibe-* kindred of both families together, as well as well-wishers to officially know that a girl had been given out in marriage. It was the custom. It must be done.

The *Igba Nkwu* – traditional wedding finally came and it was at the bride's compound. Nwakego was elaborately dressed and adorned with coral beads. She was irresistibly beautiful on that day than the previous days Obinna had seen her. Obinna saw her that day and wondered where the extra beauty came from. He never knew she was this beautiful. He who marries beauty marries trouble; he thought. He later rebuked such thought within him and concluded by saying in his mind; Obinna, see no evil, hear no evil and speak no evil, you mustn't say such things about her. The young woman is beautiful.

The custom must be followed. Nwakego sold eggs around her father's compound; this signified that the bride possessed the capability to open a shop and make money just as the custom demanded. A woman must not stay idle in her husband's home. Idleness was regarded as an evil thing.

It's evil to be idle. Was she not to contribute to the family's finance no matter how meagre her contribution could be? Being idle makes the devil visit. The devil finds work for idle hands to do. That was why young women were empowered from home before venturing into marriage.

When the guests were all gathered and relaxed for the occasion, Nwakego was given an *Iko-* wooden cup, filled with palm wine by her father. With the *Iko*, she would search for her husband who hid among the guests.

It was the custom and it must be adhered to. She was to be distracted by the guests especially the young men around while searching for her husband. She searched and searched while the expected distraction was given to her. At last, she saw him in the midst of the guests and rapturously offered the cup to him with curtsy. She first sipped the wine before giving some to her groom. After drinking, they both headed straight to the frontage in nuptial dance where traditional music enveloped the scene.

They danced with their guests who threw money around them. The marriage rites were completed that day. The bride and groom were wished joy by their various guests. The *Igba Nkwu* ended successfully in accordance to the custom.

The church wedding was exactly two months after the *Igba nkwu* – traditional wedding. It took place in the city of Eyimba-St Paul's Catholic Church Umule. It was in the month of June; a period when the cloud wept heavily with its tears falling like tiny threads from the sky to the earth. However, the prayers of the couple had the clouds kept mute. Yes, nature itself had been friendly to them. Could it have known the date of the event? No rain maker was summoned to hold the rain from crying that day.

In the church, the couple was tied in marriage by the officiating minister, Reverend Father Francis. At the exchange of marital vows, they were declared husband and wife.

I Obinna Udoka
Take you Nwakego Amadi for my lawful wife,
to have and to hold from this day forward,
for better, for worse, for richer, for poorer, in

sickness and health until Death do us part.
That was Obinna's vow.

Just immediately after the wedding, the tag on the car was changed from 'about to wed' to 'just wedded'. The new couple moved out of the church; they were driven to the reception hall where guests were waiting to receive them.

The feisty reception hall was loaded with lots of activities which were sequentially followed. Frank and Chinwe were there.

Right there was a striking act. Obinna was asked by the master of ceremony; 'Who is the one person you respect and love most in your life?'

Was it planned? He could not wait to think, but he enthusiastically answered; 'My sister.' He told the life story of his sister's acts of love. His mind flashed to the events of the past. 'My sister! My sister!' he answered.

At that moment, applause filled the hall. Chinwe couldn't believe what was happening. She wanted to laugh but couldn't laugh. The laughter couldn't just come. Was she to cry? She stood motionless and still like an unruffled runnel. The thoughts of the past flowed in and out of her mind freely. She remembered the trail of her brother's scratch of love.

She quickly searched and searched; the files of her heart. As her mind rummaged on the things of old, she dwelt in placidity. She ruminated on why her brother kept this age-long experience in his mind. Her heart had indeed searched out the files of her heart.

'My sister...' Those two words throbbed in her heart like a strong drum. It continued throbbing as if there were players drumming within her.

Obinna had a record of all events in his heart's chronicles. Now was it time to lay bare the old saga. Obinna had proved to the world that even with his wife Nwakego, Chinwe was second to none.

CHAPTER FOURTEEN

Evening came. One could hear the din emanating from cabs and motorcyclists, the hubbub from passersby who were returning from the ever busy Ariaria market, the shouts, and curses of the drivers and conductors and the rumbling of big trucks. The sounds were deafening. The city laid spy with lots of streaming activities.

Chinwe still sat on the seat with Frank by her side. Her eyes were still intensively fixed into his eyes. Frank had just touched her again. She had returned to her state of consciousness. The day had been a reminiscence of things which took place right from the cradle of her life.

Since 9:00am, her mouth had been unzipped to gush out sequentially, the thoughts which occupied her unsteady mind. Far from her mind was the thought of her childlessness in marriage. Her previous thoughts of wakeful nights had been fixed on her childlessness and the search for solution. That had always made her worried but with frank she had had an assurance of hope.

She had narrated the tales of old- her narration had been woven with sonorous moments of sadness that forced sweaty waters out of her liquid eyes. Frank had been tongue less but all ears to the congregated words that flowed out from her mouth as history- *the files of her heart.*

Frank had watched her all day. He could only empathize with her. He could also calm her down by wiping away the tears that flowed down to her cheeks.

After her narration, she became light and ebullient. She felt like a huge weight had been lifted off her chest and she was not at all narcissistic about herself.

The evening ran fast to its end. Darkness was beginning to make its total penetration, overshadowing the light. Chinwe went into her kitchen to perform her cooking duties. Just after this, she would go in to bid the day farewell in her husband's arms.

***

The day had fully disappeared as darkness covered everywhere. They had come out at night without been called, only in the day would they be lost without being stolen, what could they be? The sons of darkness; they decorate the dark sky at night with lights.

The owl hooted and hooted. It hooted in a more terrifying manner. Its hoots were inscrutable; it was quite a baffling experience. Evil must be knocking, she mumbled reflectively.

Her mind had been filled with several unimaginable thoughts. She had debated things in their rights and wrongs and had gone into the night with insoluble agitation. She suffered from insomnia for hours but as calmness descended into her mind, she was fully perked up to fall to the pleas of the night.

***

Chinwe found herself in Umuozo with Obinna. They had set out early in the morning, beaten black and blue by the angry sun. They meandered two kilometres away from the village, crossing a small river before entering into a high dense forest.

She trod the path with Obinna who looked frightful with his emaciated face and bonny body. The more they walked into the forest his look became more and more horrid. The humidity of the scene changed. It changed filling the mortal beings with goose pimples.

Chinwe felt pervaded in her body with an intolerable sense of fear. They walked more to a very long distance deep into the forest. She watched all sides. She searched and searched for the path that led them into the forest, but she could not find it again. How could she, when the whole path seemed covered and closed? The sky seemed to be touching the earth like an oversized long garment. Her senses were gripped with uncontrollable dread.

She moved clumsily with her hand clung into his hand. What were they even doing in such a place? All her life in Umuozo, she had never been to a place like this... How could she be a follower knowing not the purpose for such an adventure? What are we even doing here? She thought. She couldn't decipher, only God knew. She pestered him with an irritating question; 'Where are we even going?'

She received a snub while awaiting an answer- she got no response from him, not even a hiss. She stood still in tremor, she could not continue with the movement as her heart thumped violently, playing like an *ikolo* drum: 'Obim, please where are we? Let's go! Take me out of here, please!' she screamed.

Her screaming was immediately taken over by a rustle and fused echoes of unidentified voices which sounded thunderously. Her body jerked feverishly. Her head began to swell. It swelled as if it could burst like a balloon.

Scared to her bones, she stood watching from a stone's throw, she watched

Obinna transform apparently into a white apparel. He smiled at her. At a wink of an eye, he disappeared into the thin air.

'Obim! Where are you? Don't leave me here please! Come! Come!' Chinwe cried bitterly.

She stood shedding tremulous tears from her eyes. She was crestfallen; the goose pimples on her body became intense. She glanced a distance backwards. Behold, she saw a skeleton walking towards her direction. It walked as fast as air passing her indifferently.

Speechless, Chinwe picked a race, running relentlessly. But to where? Where does she know? The roads where covered. She saw the road covered in a clapping relationship- the firmament shook hands with the land and sealed it up with a clap. She ran. She just needed to run. She ran to no direction, her heart pounded fast. She shouted without hearing herself shouting. She could not find the path again! Everywhere was covered with sand. As she ran towards nowhere, she turned back and discovered she was being chased by the skeleton. She became immobile as the skeleton appeared before her—staring at her. She had a convergence with the skeleton. She fell down faintly with her eyes closed.

At the count of five, her eyes opened and before her now was Obinna standing. How did you get here? She thought. She wailed. 'Obim, where have you been? What is happening? I've searched for you. Why did you abandon me in this jungle of death?'

Obinna could not say a word. He walked to a little distance beside an *iroko* tree. He stood there looking at her with a direct eye contact. His eyes were red. He blinked the eyes, on and off, and they became deeper in redness. The retina seemed to be burning like candle. He bid her farewell and at this point turned into a pool of blood. This was enigmatic.

'No!' Chinwe screamed. She wept uncontrollably. Who could hear her voice? Could this be life? 'Obim! Obim! Where are you? What is going on?' she bellowed. She rolled herself on the verdant ground; weeping profusely.

She screamed and screamed yet again. As she screamed to the top of her voice she found herself conscious on the bed- in her room. She sweated profusely- the waters on her body had deeply soaked her pillows. Her breath was at its fastest, her heart throbbed like a drum played by thousands of drummers. She watched her side, alarmed. Frank was not there! But he was here by my side on the bed. He was here, just here. We slept together on the same bed. She thought.

She stood up and checked her time. It was 4:00am. She had a very long night mare. Her conscious mind took her round the house.

First, she headed to the toilet and bathroom, she couldn't find Frank there. She walked nervously to the other rooms; to the sitting room and at last to the kitchen, but frank wasn't there.

'Frank, where are you?' She called with a frightened voice.

This was unusual of him. He wasn't in any way like this. He never left the house without telling her, not at this odd hour, not even in her sleep. Something must be wrong.

She headed to her room. She gnarled herself on the bed. She was bewildered and dumbfounded into speechlessness. She took her phone and dialed frank's number:

The MTN number you're calling is currently switched off, please try again later.

She hissed. She dialed Obinna's number; the number was also switched off. She dialed Nwakego's number; the number was unavailable at the moment. Who else will she dial? Yes, her mother. She remembered. She dialed her mother's number and the response was 'network busy'. What could have happened to them? She cogitated.

She hurled herself to the bed, cried out sonorously and smashed her phone into pieces at the wall. Her mind suggested lots of evil to her. In her mind came a gentle syncopation of a dirge by unknown voices. Her head was deeply crowded by thousands of overwhelming thoughts.

What could she do? Bolt- run away? By this time of the morning? There was danger hitting and knocking at her door. She could not rationalize on the right thing to do. She must leave the house but to nowhere? Her legs were ceased in immobility like a crippled. She fell to the floor.

'What is happening? Obim! Where are you?' She deeply cried with none to wipe away her tears. She continued:

Obim, what is happening?
Obim, in my heart is your abode
Obim, my blood has ceased to flow in my
vein.
Obim, the thought of you flows there in
Like a conflagration burns my urge to see
you.
Could my tears bring you present to me?
What have you not done for me?
In my childlessness would your
love for me give me a child.
In my heart would your name be
written forever and ever
For with you does my soul find
comfort, where are you?
Could this be the long night
That invites the coming of the dawn?

Obim, where're you?

Chinwe wept bitterly. What could have happened to Obinna? Where were the others? 'Obim! Obim!' she screamed and her voice was lost in the air.

IWU JEFF (Iwuchukwu Jephta) is a poet, playwright and fiction writer. He is a teacher of English and literature with Nigerian Certificate in Education (NCE) in English (double major), and a B.A(ed) in English. His works have appeared in literary magazines and anthologies, few have garnered awards.

www.ingramcontent.com/pod-product-compliance
Lightning Source LLC
Chambersburg PA
CBHW032019170626
46807CB00006B/2869

* 9 7 8 9 7 8 9 6 4 1 8 9 5 *